Strange Spirits
of
St. Ignace

Don't miss these exciting, action-packed books by Johnathan Rand:

Michigan Chillers:

#1: Mayhem on Mackinac Island
#2: Terror Stalks Traverse City
#3: Poltergeists of Petoskey
#4: Aliens Attack Alpena
#5: Gargoyles of Gaylord
#6: Strange Spirits of St. Ignace
#7: Kreepy Klowns of Kalamazoo
#8: Dinosaurs Destroy Detroit
#9: Sinister Spiders of Saginaw
#10: Mackinaw City Mummies
#11: Great Lakes Ghost Ship
#12: AuSable Alligators
#13: Gruesome Ghouls of Grand Rapids

Freddie Fernortner, Fearless First Grader:

#1: The Fantastic Flying Bicycle
#2: The Super-Scary Night Thingy
#3: A Haunting We Will Go
#4: Freddie's Dog Walking Service
#5: The Big Box Fort
#6: Mr. Chewy's Big Adventure
#7: The Magical Wading Pool

American Chillers:

#1: The Michigan Mega-Monsters
#2: Ogres of Ohio
#3: Florida Fog Phantoms
#4: New York Ninjas
#5: Terrible Tractors of Texas
#6: Invisible Iguanas of Illinois
#7: Wisconsin Werewolves
#8: Minnesota Mall Mannequins
#9: Iron Insects Invade Indiana
#10: Missouri Madhouse
#11: Poisonous Pythons Paralyze Pennsylvania
#12: Dangerous Dolls of Delaware
#13: Virtual Vampires of Vermont
#14: Creepy Condors of California
#15: Nebraska Nightcrawlers
#16: Alien Androids Assault Arizona
#17: South Carolina Sea Creatures
#18: Washington Wax Museum
#19: North Dakota Night Dragons

Adventure Club series:

#1: Ghost in the Graveyard
#2: Ghost in the Grand
#3: The Haunted Schoolhouse

www.americanchillers.com

Johnathan Rand's

MICHIGAN CHILLERS

#6: Strange Spirits of St. Ignace

An AudioCraft Publishing, Inc. book

Book storage and warehouses provided by Chillermania!©
Indian River, Michigan

Warehouse security provided by:
Lily Munster and Scooby-Boo

Michigan Chillers #6: Strange Spirits of St. Ignace
ISBN 13-digit: 978-1-893699-11-3

Librarians/Media Specialists:
PCIP/MARC records available at www.americanchillers.com

Cover illustration by Dwayne Harris
Cover layout and design by Sue Harring

Printed in USA

Strange Spirits
of
St. Ignace

VISIT CHILLERMANIA!

WORLD HEADQUARTERS FOR BOOKS BY JOHNATHAN RAND!

CHILLERMANIA!

**I-75 Exit 313
then south
1 mile!**

Yooperland

Indian River

Alpena

Traverse City

MICHIGAN

Mt. Pleasant

Bay City

Grand Rapids

Lansing

Detroit

Kalamazoo

Visit the HOME for books by Johnathan Rand! Featuring books, hats, shirts, bookmarks and other cool stuff not available anywhere else in the world! Plus, watch the American Chillers website for news of special events and signings at *CHILLERMANIA!* with author Johnathan Rand! Located in northern lower Michigan, on I-75! Take exit 313 . . . then south 1 mile! For more info, call (231) 238-0338. And be afraid! Be veeeery afraaaaaaiiiid . . . .

1

"Well, that looks like it's the last of it. Are you all packed, Kevin?"

Dad stood next to our car, hands on his hips, gazing into the open trunk. He looked up at the duffle bags strapped on the roof.

"You bet!" I answered excitedly. "Let's go! I've been waiting for this all summer!"

The morning sky was blue and clear. A perfect day to begin our vacation. I could see some of my friends in their yards, looking wishfully toward us. They all knew what we were doing; they all wished that they could go. Even David Skinner, my best friend, said that he would give me his new football if he could go. I asked Dad, but he said no. He likes David, but he said that this was a family trip. Maybe some other time.

Dad closed the trunk and hopped into the car. We were on our way.

Camping. Not only camping, but camping up north. St. Ignace, Michigan, to be exact. St. Ignace is the first city you come to on the other side of the Mackinac Bridge. It's one of the oldest cities in Michigan. One of the first people to live there was Father Jaques Marquette. He lived there from 1666 till the time he died in 1675.

But even before that, there were other people there.

Indians.

The forest was very special to them, and there is a lot of Indian history all around St. Ignace. Camping there sure was going to be a lot of fun.

I've never been camping before. Neither has my sister, Erin, or Bobby, my younger brother.

Well, okay — we've camped in our back yard a few times. It's kind of fun. We pitch a tent and roast marshmallows, and Dad tells scary stories. Once he told us a story that was so scary, Bobby started to cry! He wouldn't spend the night in the tent with us, and wound up staying in his bed in the house that night. What a baby.

But this camping trip would be different. We would be camping in the forest — in the wild, with trees and birds and animals. I hear that there are bears in northern Michigan. I hoped I would see one!

What I didn't know was that we would see a bear all right . . . and a lot of other things that I wouldn't have believed myself . . . except the things happened to *me*, so I know they were real. Let me just say this: If you're going to spend any time in the forest, you'd better know what you're doing.

But I was prepared. I had a brand-new pocketknife, and an outdoor survival handbook. Which, at the moment, was in the hands of my sister.

"Can I *please* have my book back?" I pleaded. She'd been reading it since breakfast. I thought I was being nice by letting her borrow it, but she'd had it for an hour.

"Fine," she said, slapping the book closed and tossing it into my lap. She shook her head and rolled her eyes.

That's just like my sister. We get along well enough, but she can be pretty snappy sometimes. She's 13 . . . a year older than I am . . . so she thinks that she's the boss.

Right.

"Can I see it?" Bobby asked from his seat in

the car.

"Yeah, when I'm through," I said. "I just got it and I haven't even been able to read it myself yet." I shot a glare at Erin, and she ignored me like she usually does.

I opened the book in my lap. It's very cool. There are different sections that tell you what kinds of trees and plants and animals you'll find in the woods. It has a section on how to survive on edible plants, and how to cook them. And it shows you which plants to stay away from. There are a lot of plants in the woods that, if eaten, are very poisonous. You really have to know what you're doing if you're going to eat wild plants and berries and things. You just can't wander into the woods and start eating the first green leaf you find!

There is a lot more in the book as well. It shows you how to start a fire without any matches, how to build a lean-to, how to catch fish . . . all kinds of things. When we got to our camp site, I was going to see if I could do some of the things that were in the book.

I shoved my hand in my pocket and pulled out my knife. I had saved for it and bought it at the sporting goods store. It was a good knife, too. The handle was made of wood and had a deer carved into it. It had four different folding blades, each one a different length. The knife had taken every penny that I'd saved, but I thought it was worth it.

Of course, at the time, I didn't know just how valuable that knife was going to be . . . because soon, that pocket knife was going to save our lives.

2

The drive to St. Ignace took us about six hours. Six *boring* hours, I might add. Bobby fell asleep the minute we left the driveway, and he slept most of the way. Dad, Mom and Erin and I played some games. We made up a different name for different kinds of cars, and then when we saw one, we would call out its name. The object, of course, was to be the first to spot a car. You got a point for each one you saw, and I was doing great. I usually win at this game.

At about the half-way point, Erin and I got into a huge fight. She saw a giant semi-truck carrying six vans . . . and she counted them all as points. I was sure it had to be illegal . . . but we didn't have any rule book, so Dad said that she could count the points.

That put her four points ahead of me, and we fought about it all the way till we reached the Mackinac Bridge. Dad got so mad at Erin and I that he threatened to turn the car around and go home.

Bobby woke up just as we started across the Mackinac Bridge. Let me tell you, if you've never crossed it before, it's really something to see. It's five miles long, and hundreds of feet in the air. Boats in the water below look like tiny bugs. We even saw a big freighter passing right below us. It was cool.

But it was the other side of Mackinac Bridge that I was excited about. Because right on the other side of the bridge was St. Ignace.

We were going camping.

As we made our way across the bridge, I shoved my hand into my pocket again just to make sure my knife was still there. Then I fumbled through my outdoor survival book again, looking at the pictures and drawings. I couldn't wait.

We wouldn't be camping at a campground, either. Dad knows a man who has a lot of property not far from town. Dad says that it's nothing but forest and swamp land for miles and miles. No homes, no roads, no people—just forest. Trees and swamps. And animals and bugs and birds.

It was time for dinner, so we ate at a restaurant in St. Ignace. From where I sat, I could see ferry boats taking people across Lake Huron to Mackinac Island. Summertime sure is a busy place in St. Ignace.

After dinner, we got back in the car and started to drive. Soon, Dad turned off the highway onto a small dirt road. After a few bumpy miles, the dirt road turned into a beaten two-track. It was obvious that there hadn't been anyone back here in a long, long time.

Erin had fallen asleep, and I couldn't resist giving her a bumblebee. That's when you stick your finger right near someone's ear when they're sleeping. As you just barely touch their ear, you make a buzzing sound. Because they're sleeping, the person thinks that there's a bee in their ear.

"*Bzzzzzzz* . . . ."

Well, Erin freaked out. *Totally.* It was great! She snapped awake and slapped the side of her head to smack the 'bee' that had been 'buzzing' by her ear. It was all I could do to keep myself from laughing. When she saw the silly grin on my face, she was *hot*.

"Knock it off, Kevin!" she screamed at me. "Mom! Dad! Tell Kevin to knock it off!"

15

I quickly flipped open my outdoor survival handbook and pretended that I had been reading.

"What?" I said innocently, looking up from the book. "I've been reading. What's your problem?"

"You're going to get it," she hissed, slugging me in the shoulder. Bobby started giggling. "You too," Erin said, turning to glare at him. *"You're going to get it if you don't wipe that little smirk off your face."*

The car came to a sudden stop, and Mom and Dad opened the doors. I hopped out and looked around.

Trees. All around us was nothing but trees. The two-track road that we'd been traveling on was hardly even noticeable. It was all grown over with long green grass and small shrubs.

The sounds of the forest filled the air. There were birds and crickets, and a light *shussshhh* of wind as it crept through the trees. There were no car horns, no airplanes. No tires on pavement, no yelling on the street corner. All we could hear were the sounds of the forest.

"Okay gang," Dad said as he began lowering duffle bags from the roof of the car. "Let's get these bags unpacked."

It was total confusion for a little while. I think Dad wanted us to believe that he's a good camper, but he sure wasn't having much luck with one of the tents. The poles kept coming apart and the tent would fall down. Dad was frustrated and saying things under his breath. Mom stood by trying to help, but Dad said that he'd done this a thousand times and he could do it himself.

As for my tent, it was already up. I have a small two-person tent that I practiced setting up in the back yard of our house. That's where Erin and I would sleep. Mom, Dad, and Bobby would sleep in the bigger tent right next to ours.

That is, if Dad was able to keep it from collapsing.

Finally, just before it got dark, he got the tent up. We left a lot of gear in the car, because Dad said that we would be hiking back to another camping spot in the morning. We could leave the gear in the car for tonight, then load it into our packs in the morning.

As I lay awake in the dark tent, I thought about our trip. It was a dream come true. Here we were, camping in the wilds of northern Michigan. I had a new knife, and a new outdoor survival handbook.

This was going to be cool. The adventure of a lifetime. We were really camping. Real camping, not just backyard stuff.

In the wild forests of St. Ignace.

After a while my eyes grew heavy, and I fell asleep to the sounds of a million crickets.

How long I slept, I don't know . . . but I awoke to the sound of screaming! A shrill painful wailing pierced the darkness. It didn't take me long to figure out who it was.

Dad!

Dad was screaming at the top of his lungs! Then Mom started screaming, too! When grownups scream like that, you can be sure that whatever is happening can't be good!

3

I snapped up in my sleeping bag, and so did Erin. *What was it?!?!* I thought. *What was wrong?!?!*

A light clicked on in the tent next to us. Dad and Mom were still screaming their heads off.

Oh no! What's happened to Mom and Dad?!?! What if something happened to Bobby?!?!?

Now I could hear frantic shuffling, and in the darkness I fumbled for my pocketknife. I had set it on the floor of the tent next to my pillow. I found it instantly, and gripped it tightly. I unzipped the tent flap.

"What are you doing?!?!" Erin stammered.

"I want to know what's going on!" I said. "Mom and Dad are in trouble!"

In the next instant I had slipped out of my sleeping bag and was standing outside.

The coarse ground was cold and clammy on my feet. Gritty dirt stuck to my bare skin. I stood in front of my tent, gripping my still-folded knife, but ready to use it if I had to.

Mom and Dad were out of the tent, and they were shining their flashlight beams at one another. They looked silly like that, Dad in his pajamas and Mom in a nightgown. They were hopping up and down and brushing themselves off.

"Ouch!" Dad yelped, as he swept his hand over his chest. "There's another one!" Mom was doing the same thing.

"What's wrong?" I asked, running up to them.

"Ants!" Dad yelled, smacking his hand on his arm. "Ouch! We set up the tent on an ant's nest!"

There's a time in your life when you just want to roll over on the ground laughing. Sometimes it's just better to hold it in and not let anyone know that you're laughing inside.

This was one of those times. But I'll never forget the site of Mom and Dad in the glow of the flashlight beams, hopping up and down like bunnies gone crazy, brushing ants off each other.

Somehow, Bobby slept right through the whole ordeal. The ants hadn't bothered him (I would tease him later about not being tasty enough). Regardless, Mom and Dad had to wake him up so that they could move the tent to another place. A place without ants.

Finally, after about an hour of stumbling and fumbling in the dark, Mom and Dad had moved the tent and went back to sleep.

But I was wide awake.

I found my small pen light, clicked it on inside my sleeping bag, and opened my outdoor survival handbook. It was so cool. There was so much to learn about the outdoors, so much to make and do. I really hoped that I would have a chance to make some of the things in the book. Maybe I could even find the right kind of plants and berries to eat. The book said that this was the season for blueberries, so I was going to be on the lookout for those.

After a while, I grew tired and was able to fall asleep.

When I awoke in the morning, I was the first up. I climbed out of the tent and stood. It was real early, and the sky was a rich, bright pink. Birds were singing, and the air was fresh and sweet. The sun would be up in a few minutes.

I was about to gather up some dead branches

for the morning fire, but when I looked at the ground, I stopped.

There were strange tracks on the ground. Not just tracks, but *animal* tracks. *Huge* ones.

I kneeled down to the ground. The tracks were big . . . bigger than my hand. And they were definitely animal tracks. I stood up and followed them around our campsite. Whatever it was, it had been all over our campsite during the night!

I followed the tracks around and around . . . and they led right to the door of Mom and Dad's tent!

"Mom?" I whispered hoarsely. "Dad? Are you guys all right?"

I heard shuffling inside the tent.

"Yeah, fine," I heard Dad say groggily. "Why?"

"There are tracks all over the place out here," I said, looking down at the prints in the ground.

"Probably a raccoon," Dad said from inside the tent. I heard more shuffling, and he unzipped the tent flap and stepped out into the cool morning air. Dad's got these silly striped pajamas that look ridiculous. But I wouldn't tell him that!

He looked at the tracks on the ground. "No, these definitely aren't raccoon tracks. I think these are bear tracks."

Holy cow! A bear had been walking right

through our camp site! Cool! I wish I had been awake to see it!

Erin was awake now, and she came out of the tent. Mom and Bobby were stirring as well. They all came out to see the big tracks that criss-crossed our camp site.

"He was looking for something to eat," Dad said. "It's a good thing we left the food in the car and not in the tents. He would have torn everything to shreds to get at it."

"But what will we do when we can't keep the food in the car?" Erin asked.

Good question.

"We'll throw a rope over a tree branch, tie all of our food up, and pull it up into the air. That way, the bear can't reach it."

I'd heard of that trick before. It made sense. At least, more sense than setting your tent up on an ant's nest.

But there was something strange about these bear tracks. I couldn't put my finger on it right away, but I knew there was something odd about them.

I was in charge of making the morning fire, and, after breakfast, we packed everything up and broke camp. All of us had backpacks. Even Bobby.

He couldn't carry much, but he had a little pack and was excited about carrying it. Dad locked up the car, made a check of the site, and we started to walk along the old two-track.

We were on our way.

We walked for what seemed like hours. Erin got tired and started to whine about it. I was tired, too, but I kept my mouth shut. I was surprised at Bobby. For as young as he was, he held out great. He walked right along behind me, whistling and humming most of the day. He only complained a couple of times.

Finally, when we reached a small stream, Dad decided that it was time to stop for the night.

We set up camp, and Dad was careful to make sure that there were no ants around. I don't think he wanted to go through what he did the night before.

After the tents were up, Dad built a fire and we roasted hot dogs. They were great. Mom promised us that, after it got dark, we could roast marshmallows before we went to bed.

Erin and Bobby and I had the task of washing the dinner plates. There wasn't much to wash, because we had cooked the hot dogs on sticks. All we had to wash were some cups and a few plates. But I hate washing the dishes, anyway.

We took the dishes to the stream, and it was there that I noticed the tracks — *the same tracks we'd seen this morning at the other camp site!*

"Erin, look," I said, pointing to the mud near the stream. "Look . . . these are the same tracks we saw this morning!"

Erin bent down and peered at the tracks. "I just hope he stays away from us," she said.

"Wanna go find him?" I asked.

"What?!?!" Erin cried out. "You want to go look for a bear?!?!"

"Come on," I urged. "It'll be fun. We'll stay away from him. A long ways. I promise."

Erin bit her lower lip, thinking for a moment. "Well, only if we don't go far," she said finally. "I don't think Mom and Dad would want us going very far from camp."

I went back to my tent and grabbed my outdoor survival handbook and walked back to where the stream was. I opened the handbook to the section on animal tracks.

"Look at this," I said to Erin. "Take a look at these tracks." Erin looked at the drawings of tracks in the handbook. "Now look at *these* tracks," I said, pointing to the mud.

"Yeah? So?" she began. "They're bear tracks, just like Dad said."

"But look closer, Erin," I said. "Look at the tracks in the mud. *They have six claws. The tracks in the mud have six claws . . . the ones in my handbook only have five.*"

Erin shuddered. "That's weird," she said. "I'm not sure I want to go looking for a six-clawed bear."

"Oh, come on," I said.

Suddenly, another voice spoke up. "Where we going, you guys?"

Bobby.

"We're going for a walk to look for the terrible six-clawed bear," I said. As I spoke, I raised my hands and made claws. Bobby's eyes got huge. "I wanna go!" he said excitedly.

"All right," I answered. "But you have to be quiet. Six-clawed bears don't like noises. Especially noises made by little Bobbies."

And with that, we were off. The sun was still above the trees, and there was still a few good hours of light left. We followed the strange six-clawed tracks as they wound along the stream. Then, they took a turn and went though a swamp. Soon, we came to the edge of a dark forest. The trees grew tall and thick. The tracks led into the forest.

"I think we should go back," Erin said. "It'll be dark soon. Mom and Dad aren't going to want us out after dark."

"Yeah, you're right," I said. "Let's head back."

I was about to turn and begin walking back when Bobby's hand suddenly shot out.

"Look!" he squealed.

I looked in the direction that he was pointing, and all of a sudden, I saw it.

Not forty feet away.

A bear.

He was standing near a tree . . . and he was looking right at us!

I froze.

Erin froze.

Bobby froze.

In the growing darkness, we could see the huge shape of the bear. I could see his ears, his nose, and his open mouth.

And I could see his teeth. They were absolutely huge . . . the biggest, nastiest teeth I had ever seen. It was incredible!

But what happened next I couldn't believe. *Right before our eyes the bear vanished! He disappeared while we were watching him!* He turned a strange misty white, and then . . . he was gone. It was like he evaporated into thin air.

Just like that.

"D-d-d . . . did . . . y-y-you just s-s-see that?"

Erin stammered.

"*Holy cow,*" I whispered. *"That bear just disappeared right before our eyes!"*

"Neat-o!" Bobby said. "I got to see a bear disappear!" Bobby was too young to realize that what we had just witnessed was really crazy. Bobby probably thought all bears could just vanish like that.

"Let's go," Erin said. "I don't like this. I don't like this at all."

I wasn't going to argue.

I turned and looked at the ground to follow our tracks through the swamp. The sun was now almost completely beneath the trees, and it had grown darker within the past few minutes.

But when I looked to find our tracks, they were *gone!* When we walked through the swamp the first time, our feet left big imprints in the soft earth. Now they had *vanished!* Our tracks had vanished — just like the strange bear.

We trudged through the swamp, searching for our footprints.

"They have to be around here somewhere," I said.

But the farther we walked, the more I began to realize that we might have a problem. The woods had grown dark, and all I had was a small pen light. I clicked it on and swept the ground. I still couldn't find our tracks.

Erin said it first. I hadn't wanted to hear the words, even though I had thought them.

"Kevin . . . are we . . . are we . . . *lost?*" she asked.

That's the word I didn't want to hear.

Lost.

Tears welled up in Bobby's eyes, and he began to cry. "Are we lost?" he sniffled.

"No, we're fine," I assured him. "We're not lost. We'll be back at our camp in no time."

But the fact was, I knew better.

We *were* lost. We were lost in a forest.

"Okay, let's stay calm," Erin said, but her words weren't very convincing. Her voice trembled as she spoke, and I knew she was frightened.

"What we need to do is—"

I stopped in mid-sentence.

Crunch.

I heard a noise in the woods. We were in complete darkness now, and a half moon was beginning to creep up over the trees. Bright white stars blanketed a pitch black sky.

Crunch. It was closer.

31

Erin and Bobby and I huddled together.

Crunch. Cru-crunch. Crunch. The crunching was loud, like something heavy was making them.

Like a bear.

The closer the noise came, the tighter Bobby and Erin and I huddled together. Whatever it was, it was only a few feet from us.

I held my breath. What could it be? There was something coming toward us, crunching through the underbrush.

What if it *was* the bear? What if he was looking for food? What if . . . *we were his supper?!?!*

"What is it?" Erin's whisper trembled in my ear.

"I don't know," I answered, *"but I'm going to find out."* Bravely, I reached into my pocket and pulled out my pocketknife, along with my pen light.

"What are you going to do?" Erin whispered.

"You'll see," I said.

And with that, I opened up my knife, ready for action. I drew a deep breath, held out my pen light, aimed it in the direction of the noise—and turned it on.

6

There was nothing there! I mean . . . *nothing!* It was impossible! We had heard the heavy crunching come closer and closer . . . there *had* to be something there.

Perhaps that was the scariest of all. I was sure that we would see something in the beam of the flashlight. I absolutely *knew* we would. But when I clicked the light on — *nothing.*

"Where did it go?" Erin asked.

"I wanna see the bear," Bobby pleaded.

"Well, whatever it was, it's gone now," I said.

I swept the tiny flashlight beam over ferns and brush. Long, dark shadows leapt away, but there was no sign of any animal.

Nothing.

I forgot about the noise. Right now we had a

bigger problem: we were lost. We were lost in the forest.

At *night*.

I took charge. "Okay," I said boldly. "First off, let's not get any more lost than we already are. We'll stay right here. Sooner or later Mom and Dad will come looking for us."

"But it's getting colder," Erin said. She crossed her arms and rubbed her shoulders with her hands.

She was right. It had gotten colder since the sun went down.

I flipped open my outdoor survival handbook. It showed a couple different ways to start a fire without matches. One way was by making a bow and using a spindle. The idea was to use the bow to make the wood spindle move real fast, and the friction created could start a fire. That looked hard.

Another way was by using flint and steel, but where would we find flint—or steel, for that matter—in the middle of the forest?

But I did have another idea. I've often smacked two rocks together and watched them make sparks . . . maybe I could do the same now.

"You guys stay right here," I said, sweeping

the penlight over the ground. "I'm going to see if I can find two rocks to bang together."

I searched and searched. I found a lot of rocks, but when I smacked them together, nothing happened.

This was *not* looking good. I decided that I would have to try the bow and spindle method, after all.

I pulled out my knife — and dropped it.

But a strange thing happened when it hit the ground. It clanked on a rock — and gave off a spark! Holy cow!

I kneeled down and found the knife, and picked up the rock that it had hit. I clicked off my penlight, and, holding my knife in my right hand, I struck it against the rock.

About a half-dozen yellow sparks flew! Maybe it would work!

"Hey guys!" I said, walking back to Erin and Bobby. They were huddled together beneath a cedar tree. "I think I've got it!"

"Yeah, well maybe you can get a shot for it," Erin sneered.

That's my sister for you.

"We need to crush up some dried leaves and grass," I said. "Crush it and tear it till it's really fine.

We need something to catch a spark."

We all got to work. There were dried leaves and grass all around us, so we didn't have to hunt. Then I cleared out a small area to build a fire. I pulled away all of the brush and branches so that when the fire started, it wouldn't catch anything else on fire.

That is, *if* we could get a fire started.

Erin and Bobby stood anxiously by as I knelt down and pulled my pocketknife and the rock out of my pocket. I clicked off the pen light, wanting to save as much of the batteries as I could. I struck the handle of my pocketknife against the rock.

Crack! Tiny yellow sparks exploded, scattered, and disappeared.

Crack! Again, yellow sparks sprang out. I could see a few of them landing in the dry tinder, but so far, nothing else happened. I blew gently on some of the sparks that landed in the dry grass and leaves, but a fire didn't take.

Crack! Again, the same thing.

Crack! Nothing. This wasn't as easy as it looked in the book. I kept hitting the handle of my knife against the rock. Sparks flew, and suddenly —

One caught! The tiny yellow bead landed in the tinder. I blew on it very gently, ever so softly.

The yellow spot began to grow and grow, turning orange as it spread in the dry grass and leaves. Suddenly, a small flame appeared! I blew a little bit more, spreading the flame through the brittle, dry fibers. Other leaves began to catch, and the flames began to flicker higher.

"You did it!" Erin shouted. Her voice echoed through the dark forest. "You really did it!"

"Quick!" I exclaimed, jumping to my feet. "Find some tiny twigs and branches! Some real dead, dry ones!"

As the tiny flames grew, I placed small sticks and branches on top of the burning tinder. The small branches caught, and I placed a few larger branches in. I could already feel the comforting warmth of the fire as the flames continued to grow. Bobby and Erin drew closer, warming themselves by the fire.

I was feeling better, and even a bit proud of myself. Even though we were lost, we had been able to start a fire without any matches. All we would have to do was wait till morning when it was light, and I was sure we would be able to find our way out of here. Or Mom and Dad would find us. We were going to be okay.

Or so I thought. Things were about to get

really strange.

And *scary*.

Erin noticed it first. The three of us had been huddled around the fire, and we hadn't paid much attention to the forest around us.

"Kevin!" she suddenly whispered. *"Look!"*

I turned to see what she was looking at, and a wave or terror swept through my body like a freight train. I gasped.

Because all around us, in the dark shadows, behind trees and branches, were eyes. Not just one pair, but dozens. They were glowing, reflecting in the yellow firelight. Some were bigger than others, some were smaller.

But one thing was for certain—they were all looking . . . *at us!!!*

7

They were everywhere. I tried to count them, but there were just too many. Whatever they were — animals, I figured — they were just far enough into the shadows that we couldn't see them.

What could they be? Bears? Deer? Giant raccoons? There were all kinds of animals in the forest . . . I wasn't even sure what kind or how many. Where we live, we see a few raccoons now and then. But that's about it, besides birds and stray dogs and cats.

"Are they going to eat us?" Bobby asked.

"Of course not," I answered quickly.

But deep down, I wasn't so sure.

Then we could hear the crunching of branches. The animals — whatever kind they were — began to move! I could see their eyes moving in the dark. Some came closer, some went farther away. Some of their eyes were so close that I could actually see them blinking in the light of the fire . . . but I still couldn't see the shape or size of the animal.

Just their sinister eyes, glaring back at us in the darkness.

"I'm s-s-s-scared," Bobby stammered. He started to cry, and Erin put her arm around him and drew him close.

"We'll be fine," she said. "They're just animals. They're curious. They aren't going to hurt us."

I hoped Erin was right. I had read stories about animals with rabies, and how they can get really crazy. They go mad, sometimes attacking things like trees or lawnmowers. I saw on the news one time about a rabid dog that even attacked a fire hydrant!

Thinking about things like that, I began to frighten myself.

Stop it, I thought. *Don't think about stuff like that. They're just wild animals, and they're probably just curious, like Erin said.*

Besides . . . I had to show Erin and Bobby that I wasn't afraid. If they knew that I wasn't afraid, then they wouldn't be afraid, either.

"They're just animals," I said boldly. "I can probably scare them away myself." I stood up and waved my arms. "Hey you!" I shouted to the glaring pairs of yellow eyes. "Get outta here! Go on! Go home!"

Wait a minute, I thought. *They are home. This is their home.*

"Go . . . someplace else!" I yelled.

It was working! Pair by pair, the eyes began to disappear! They were leaving. I felt strong and brave.

"And don't come back!" I shouted confidently, shaking my fist into the air. "Stay away, or you'll be sorry! I have an outdoor survival handbook, you know!"

I was certain the animals couldn't understand what I was saying, but just shouting those words made me feel better, like I had some special power over the creatures.

I turned to face Erin and Bobby, still huddled close around the fire.

"See?" I said proudly. "Just animals. They're gone now."

But they weren't watching me. Erin and Bobby were staring up, above the flames of the fire, into the rising smoke. Tiny orange sparks drifted up into the air and went out, and the smoke whirled and danced as it floated up.

It was then that I saw what Bobby and Erin were staring at.

I dropped my pocketknife. I dropped my outdoor survival handbook. I couldn't do anything but stare.

In the smoke, just above the fire, an enormous face was appearing.

A face . . . in the smoke!

It was the strangest thing I had ever seen in my life.

It was a face. A real face in the smoke. It wasn't just smoke that *looked* like a face . . . it was an actual face that was forming in the gray wisps of smoke. I could see a chin and a nose and a mouth. As I watched, the face became even clearer.

Erin and Bobby were huddled close together on the other side of the fire. I could see them staring up at the huge face that loomed over the fire. They were terrified.

I was, too, I guess.

I took a step back. Then another. The face was complete now, and I could make it out perfectly. In the glow of the fire, the smoke looked eerie and strange. But for the first time, I could see exactly what — or who — it was.

It was the face of an old Indian! Smoke had formed lines on his face and forehead. His face was as clear as a picture on a postcard, except I could see through the smoke. The giant, gray face hung above our campfire, glaring at us.

And he didn't look very pleased with us.

Slowly, I took another step back.

"*STOP!*" the face in the smoke boomed.

It spoke to me! Holy cow! The face in the smoke could talk!

And I wasn't going to argue. Not with the talking gray face of an Indian made out of smoke!

"*What are you doing here!?!?!*" the face in the smoke demanded. As his mouth moved, wisps of smoke swirled and twisted and floated away. When I didn't answer, the face spoke again, only much louder this time.

"*WHAT ARE YOU DOING HERE?!?!?*" The thundering voice echoed through the dark night. Erin and Bobby and I all flinched.

"Ah, ummm . . . um . . ." I didn't know what to say. I've never talked to a face made out of smoke before.

When I didn't say anything more, the face in the smoke suddenly grew angry. It drew back and lurched forward, and the next thing I knew, it was

44

right in front of my nose! Smoke licked at my face, and I could smell the thick stench of burned wood. I winced and held my breath.

"Do you know where you are?" the face asked. His voice was calmer now, quieter.

I shook my head. "N-no," I managed to stammer. "I-I mean, I know we're in the woods. Somewhere near St. Ignace."

The old face drew back a little bit, and I relaxed a little. I shot a glance at Erin and Bobby. They were still huddled close on the other side of the fire. Erin had both arms around Bobby, and Bobby had both hands over his eyes. Every second or two he would slowly spread his fingers, take a peek, then quickly close his fingers.

The old Indian spoke. "Yes, indeed, you are near St. Ignace," the strange face said. "But do you know what is happening around you?"

I was having a hard time believing what I was seeing. I've seen some pretty strange things before, but nothing like this. I shook my head from side to side without speaking.

"Avan-Dar, is returning," the mysterious face said. "Avan-Dar and his terrible spirits are coming back. They are coming back, and no one can stop them. You must leave. Quickly."

"But . . . but we're lost," I said. "We don't know—"

"YOU MUST LEAVE NOW!" the old Indian boomed. "Avan-Dar is far too powerful. You must leave!" His voice was more forceful, and I flinched.

But then the face began to disappear. It began to drift off, and little wisps of smoke twirled up into the starry sky. Orange sparks from the fire carried the gray smoke into the darkness.

"WAIT!" I cried. "Don't go! Who is Avan-Dar?!?!? How do we get out of here?!?!?"

But it was too late. As I spoke those last words, the last of the old Indian's face had simply faded up into the sky, billowed by the heat of the roaring fire. He was gone. The face in the smoke was gone . . . but things were about to get worse.

I looked into the darkness that surrounded our camp fire—and saw a pair of eyes.

Then another pair.

Then another.

And I knew. I knew now that the eyes didn't belong to animals.

They belonged to spirits. They belonged to spirits . . . and they were all around us!

9

One by one, pairs of eyes began to blink all around us. First there were only a few, then there were dozens. Glaring eyes, reflecting the light of the fire, watched us from the darkness. Erin held Bobby tightly, and Bobby kept his hands up over his eyes.

"I don't wanna see," he said. "Make them go away again."

I shouted at the unseen creatures. I picked up my pocketknife from the ground, flipped open a blade, and waved it around. I waved my hands, I shined the pen light at them. Nothing worked, and the tiny beam from my flashlight wasn't even strong enough to illuminate the animals — or whatever they were.

Then I realized that I hadn't been the one to scare them away the first time.

It had been the face. The face of the old Indian in the smoke is what frightened them off the first time. Maybe the creatures were afraid of the face.

Or the fire! Maybe they were afraid of fire!

There was a large stick in the fire with an end poking out. I grabbed the end that wasn't burning and pulled it out of the flames. I held it above my head like a sword.

"Go away!" I shouted. "Go away now!"

I heard gasping and heavy breathing, and mumbling.

Wait a minute! I thought. *Mumbling?!?! Did I hear mumbling?!?!?*

I took a step away from the fire and toward the pairs of eyes that still stared menacingly at us.

"Be careful," Erin whispered. I hardly heard her.

Then I heard a voice!

"It *is* you," someone—or *something*—said.

An animal? Animals can't talk!

But what if . . . what if these weren't animals? What if they were what the old Indian had said? What if they were *spirits?*

I held the burning stick high above my head. "I'm warning you," I shouted loudly. "Leave!

Leave now!"

Then, from the darkness, more gasping.

"It is him!" something shouted. The voice was a high-pitched squeal . . . the sound that you'd expect an animal to make. That is, of course, if animals could talk. But they can't.

"HAIL TO THE KING!" another voice boomed loudly.

And suddenly, all around us, the creatures of the night began to show themselves—but I wasn't prepared for what I was about to see . . . .

Spirits.

That's the only way I could describe them. They came from all around, slowly creeping toward us and showing themselves in the firelight.

They were animals! Well, sort of. They were all wispy and white, like the face in the smoke. In fact, that's what these creatures looked like! Smoke creatures!

I took a step back, still holding the burning stick high into the air. As the creatures came closer, I could make them out. I could see a bear, a porcupine, a deer, another bear, and a very large fox.

But they all seemed to be made of smoke! As they drew closer to the light of the fire, I could see them better. I could see right through them! Their eyes glowed in the firelight, but their bodies were all a hazy gray.

Like smoke. I have never . . . and probably never will . . . see anything like them again.

"HAIL TO THE KING!" the bear shouted. At this, all of the animals bowed their heads. "Hail to the King!" the animals spoke in unison.

Huh? 'King?' Who was 'King?'

One by one, the strange creatures raised their heads.

"We knew you'd come back," a deer said. "We just knew you would."

I'm sure you can imagine how strange it was, standing near a fire in the middle of the forest, surrounded by animals that were made out of smoke. And they could talk! Too freaky.

"Yes," another animal chimed in. "And just in time, too."

"What do you mean?" I finally managed to ask. I had no clue what they were talking about.

"Why, your return, of course. We have waited for you to come back, oh great King." At this, the animals bowed their heads again. "Hail to the King!" they said again.

This whole thing suddenly seemed very silly. They were worshiping *me!* They had me confused with someone else. I've never been a king before. I hadn't planned on becoming one.

"I'm afraid you're mistaken," I said. "I'm not a king. I never have been. My name is Kevin. And over there is my sister, Erin, and my little brother, Bobby."

I pointed to the two figures sitting near the fire. Bobby's hands were still over his eyes, and he spread his fingers apart just enough to catch a quick glance, then closed his fingers again.

"Your Highness, certainly you must know," a rather large raccoon said. "That is why you are here. The legend says that the King must return and lead the forest spirits into battle."

I shook my head. "I'm sorry," I said, shaking my head back and forth. "I'm not the guy. You must be looking for someone else."

All of the animals shook their heads.

"Look," the bear called out to the other animals. "Look at the knife he carries! That's proof that he is our king!"

I was still holding my pocketknife in one hand, and I held it up. I couldn't understand how a pocketknife would 'prove' that I was somehow a king.

Still holding the burning stick into the air, I

glanced down and looked at my knife.

    Holy cow!

My pocketknife! It had changed!

I don't know how, but my pocketknife had been completely transformed! It was now *twice* the size it had been! It was long and silver and shiny, and the handle was made of dark wood. At the base of the handle was a carved skull. The skull was white and looked like it might have been carved out of bone.

A low murmur of shock and surprise rumbled through the group of animals. Or spirits, or whatever they were. I just stared at the knife.

It was beautiful. Yellow and orange flames reflected from the shiny, long blade. Up until now, I'd only seen knives like this in catalogs or glass cases. Now I actually held one in my hands. It was a lot bigger than my pocketknife . . . and a lot heavier, too. There was no way I would be able to put *this* knife into my pocket!

"You see!" the bear said. "He has the knife! It is him! The King of Fire has returned!" Once again, all of the animals bowed their heads toward me. "ALL HAIL THE KING OF FIRE!" they shouted. "LONG LIVE THE KING!"

The King of Fire?!?!?

I looked at the stick I was holding. The end burned brightly, and the tip glowed hot orange. Tiny sparks flew off and drifted up into the air.

Truthfully, I guess I was enjoying the attention, however strange it was. I've never been a king before, or anything of the sort. I was president of a club that my friends and I had, but that was it. Certainly no one had ever bowed down before me.

And no one had ever, ever called me a king before! I smiled and glanced around at the animals. Maybe I could get used to being a king!

Suddenly, another murmur swept through the gathering of animal spirits. Only this time, it was a murmur of alarm.

One by one, the creatures slowly backed off into the darkness. They began to disappear, slinking off into the shadows.

"What's wrong?" I asked, glancing around as

the animals vanished into the darkness. "What's the matter?"

Then, without turning around, I knew what was happening. The old Indian. The face in the smoke. I knew he had returned. After all, that is what had scared away the animals the first time.

I turned to face the fire, expecting to see the old Indian's face swirling in a cloud of smoke.

There was a face there, all right . . . but it wasn't the smokey face of the Indian. The face that I saw in the fire was the most grotesque, scariest face that I had ever seen in my life.

Wicked.

It's the only word I could use to describe the face that I saw. Completely *wicked*.

It was a face — a face made out of fire. It had features that looked to be half-man, half animal. Its nose was long, and its mouth was open, showing jagged, uneven teeth. And its eyes were like gaping, dark holes, staring back at me from the flames in the fire.

I was terrified. I had been scared when I saw the old Indian's face, but it was nothing compared to the fear I was feeling now. The old Indian didn't seem to want to hurt me . . . but the creature I was seeing now looked like it wanted to *devour* me!

I took a big step back as the face continued to twist and turn in the flickering flames. It spun around in a circle, looking at Erin and Bobby. Then it spun back around and glared at me. It truly was the nastiest face I had ever seen.

Then, it spoke. Actually, it didn't really speak. It *hissed*. It hissed like a snake.

"*Ssssoooooo,*" it began. "*You have returned, after all. Didn't learn your lesson the first time, did you?*" It smiled an evil smile and lurched out toward me.

The first time? I thought. *What was he talking about?* I took another big step back.

"I don't know what you mean," I said loudly. "But if I were you, I wouldn't come any closer. I'm warning you. Stay away from me and my brother and my sister."

Hearing this, the face burst out laughing. It was a terrible, throaty laugh that sent shudders down my spine. Bobby screamed and so did Erin.

"*You?!?!? You think YOU have the power to threaten ME?!?!?*" Once again, thundering laughter shook the entire forest. "*How dare you try to threaten me with your silly little demand. I will do whatever I wish to do with you! And right now, I wish to do away with you! I'll do away with all THREE of you!*"

I wasn't sure what he meant by 'do away with', but I knew one thing: it wasn't going to be good.

The face reared back and up, growing larger. It opened its mouth wide, and I could see sharp, ugly teeth and a swirling, smokey tongue. If Erin and Bobby hadn't been seeing the same thing, I would have been sure that I was dreaming.

The face looked down at me and smiled that strange, nasty smile.

And then I heard a tiny voice.

It came from behind me, in the darkness. It was a quiet, meek voice.

"Raise your knife," it said. *"Show him your knife. Let him know you have the knife."*

I spun for a split instant to see who was speaking, but it was too dark. All I could see were shadows.

I turned back around to confront the terrible face in the fire. I didn't know how showing my knife would do anything to stop the hideous face that was coming closer and closer, but it was worth a shot.

Grasping the knife tightly, I thrust it up. Now, both my hands were raised into the air. In one hand I held the burning stick, and in the other, I held the knife.

The face in the fire drew back. Not only did it draw back, but an expression of fear suddenly came upon him. Fear turned to anger as he spoke.

"YOU!" he hissed. "You will not win this time! This time, I will be the victor! I will rule the Realm of the Underforest! I will be the victor, and all of the spirits will be MINE . . . including . . . YOURS!"

He was shouting now, and his voice sounded like a freight train. "LET THE BATTLE BEGIN!"

He was furious! I could see it in his eyes and in his face. Anger boiled in the yellow and orange flames.

Then, just as the old Indian face had done, he began to vanish. His face became faint and his features slipped away. The creature—whatever it was— disappeared, carried up and away by the rising smoke and sparks. I watched as he faded completely out of sight, then I turned back around.

Some of the spirit-creatures had returned, and more were reappearing from the shadows even as I watched.

I looked at the knife in my hand. Wherever it came from, it was obviously very powerful. I rolled it over in my hands, being careful not to cut myself on the razor sharp edges. I couldn't figure out how my pocketknife had changed into this huge, silver dagger.

"See," a voice behind me said. "You *are* the King of Fire. You've come back. You've come back to save us all."

I turned to see a crowd of wispy, white animals gathering. They were all looking at me.

I shook my head. "I have no idea who you're talking about. My name is Kevin Barnes. I'm not a king. I never have been. And I don't know where this knife came from. I have no idea how to 'save you all' or what I'm supposed to save you from."

"But you must," a deer said to me. "Even the wicked sorcerer Avan-Dar fears you. Did you see how he ran when you showed him who you really were?" All of the other spirits nodded their heads.

"He thinks he can defeat you, but deep down,

he knows he can't win," a possum said.

"I'm sorry," I said. "I'm still very confused. I've never heard of this . . . this 'Avan-Dar' before. I'm not who you think I am."

"Oh, but you are," the bear spoke up. "You are the King of Fire. You must help us. I'm afraid you have no other choice."

"What do you mean 'I don't have any other choice'? I haven't done anything!"

"Oh, yes you have," the raccoon said. "By showing Avan-Dar the Knife of Eternal Fire, you let him know that you were preparing for war. Even now, all of the wicked spirits are preparing to go to war — against all of us."

"What's the 'Knife of Eternal Fire'?" I asked. "And what does 'eternal' mean."

An owl that had been sitting in a tree spoke up. I hadn't seen her until now.

"Eternal means forever," she said. "The Knife of Eternal Fire was given to you exactly one hundred thousand years ago. You used it to defeat the wicked sorcerer Avan-Dar. You banished him for one hundred thousand years to the Swamp of Doom. Now his one hundred thousand years are up . . . and he is free to roam the earth."

Right. Like I was going to believe *that*.

But then again . . . what else was there to believe?

Erin and Bobby had been silent for a while, and now Erin got up and walked to my side. Bobby stayed seated where he was, his hands over his face, his eyes peering between cracks in his fingers.

"We aren't who you think we are," Erin said. "We were camping with our Mom and Dad. We got lost. That's how we wound up here. My brother isn't a king any more than I am Cleopatra."

"Who is Cleopatra?" the bear asked.

"She's the queen of the Nile," Erin answered matter-of-factly.

"What is the 'Nile'?" the bear asked.

"Never mind," Erin said. "It's just that . . . well, Kevin is right. He's not a king. And we definitely do not want to be in any war."

"It's too late for that," the deer said. "It's already begun. The battle between the good and evil spirits of the forest has started . . . and only you can help us win." The deer nodded toward me.

"Will you help us?" a raccoon pleaded.

I was silent. I stood watching the gathering of animals. Or spirits of animals, or whatever they were. They sure were a strange bunch.

But the way they looked at me made me feel

sorry for them. They seemed helpless. It was as if they really needed me.

But I'm not their king, I told myself. *I'm just a kid. A kid who's lost in the woods. How can I help them?*

Nevertheless, when I looked into their eyes, I didn't have a choice. They looked so helpless. I knew that I had to help.

"Okay," I said reluctantly. "I'll help. But I really don't know what I can do."

I had no idea what I was getting myself into — but in two seconds, I was about to find out.

A noise came from the sky.

At first it was like a distant airplane, just a light buzzing sound that was hardly noticeable. Then it grew louder and the sound grew deeper.

"What's that?" I asked. Erin, Bobby, myself, and all of the spirit-animals were looking up into the air. The owl was the first to speak.

"It's Avan-Dar's army!" she hooted. A wave of terror swept through the animals. "They're attacking already!"

The spirit animals began to scatter. One by one, they quickly vanished into the forest, except for a single raccoon. He really looked kind of odd. Since he was all gray and white, it was hard to see where his black mask was. He looked sort of like a white badger with dirt around his eyes.

"Follow me!" he shouted, and turned and began to run.

Bobby was still sitting by the fire with his hands over his eyes. Erin looked at me. I looked back at her.

"Well?" she said.

We didn't have any choice. The noise was growing louder by the second. It sounded like an army was flying in.

"Let's go," I shouted. "Bobby! Come on!"

Bobby shuffled to his feet and he bounced around the fire to where we were. The raccoon had already started to run.

"Hurry!" it said, turning for just a moment to glance back at the three of us.

And so we ran. It was awfully hard, running through the dark like that. The burning stick didn't provide much light, and I still held the knife in my other hand, so I couldn't grab my pen light. It wouldn't have been much help, anyway. Nor did I have time to grab my outdoor survival manual. It was still laying on the ground where I left it at the fire.

Unseen branches smacked at my face as we plodded through the dense, dark forest. The raccoon spirit, or whatever he was called, was right in front of us. I could just barely see his creamy white form glowing in the underbrush.

"Hurry!" he encouraged. "We must make it in time. We must hide before they get here!"

I don't know how far we ran through the dark forest. The only thing I kept thinking about was that we were probably getting farther and farther away from camp — and Mom and Dad. We would be more than lost . . . we would be *completely* lost.

Of course, if we had to fight an army of wicked spirits, then that could pose its own set of problems!

Suddenly, the raccoon we had been following slipped between the cracked roots of an old tree. The opening was very small . . . certainly not big enough for Erin, or Bobby or myself to creep through.

"Hey, uh, Mr. Raccoon?" I panted frantically, bending down to peer between the roots. It was very dark and hard to see. My burning stick now only had orange embers at the end, and didn't provide much light. There was no sign of the creature.

"Mr. Raccoon?" I asked again. "Where do we go? Where can we hide?"

But there was no answer from within the tree.

The sky above was filled with the sound of screeching and flapping wings.

"Where are they all?" Erin asked.

I wished she wouldn't have asked that question. In fact, I wished we would have stayed back at the camp, and hadn't followed those bear tracks. And right now, I wished that I hadn't looked up!

15

What I saw was the craziest creature—or spirit, or whatever you want to call it—that I'd ever seen. Like the animals, it had a smokey appearance, and it looked like I could see right through it. It hung in the air just above the treetops, and it was HUGE! It looked like some half-man, half-animal creature.

But it hadn't spotted us yet! It hovered in the air, looking skyward, searching for something.

And then we saw them. A wisp of white suddenly flew over the tree tops, then another. And another. More. Soon, dozens of white spirits were whizzing past, just above the trees. They roared by, and it sounded like a windstorm as they swept overhead.

"Holy cow," I whispered.

Erin gulped.

"Big buggies!" Bobby cried out excitedly, pointing skyward.

"They're *not* bugs," I replied. "They're not bugs at all. Shhh."

We watched as the spirits continued to fly above us. They seemed to be on their way somewhere, and weren't paying too much attention to what was on the ground. It was a good thing, too, because we didn't have anyplace to hide.

Soon, we began to see fewer and fewer spirits. The noise died down, and we spotted a few stragglers—ones who hadn't kept up with the rest of the army. In a few more minutes the sky was clear, and all we saw were stars.

"What were those things?" Erin asked.

I shook my head. "I don't know, and I'm not sure if I want to find out."

"Buggies," Bobby said.

"They aren't *bugs*," I told him again. I looked around. In the darkness, I could see the black shadows of tree trunks—nothing else. All of the animals had disappeared. The noise from the flying spirits was gone, too. The night was quiet.

"Now what?" Erin asked.

"I don't know," I said.

"Well, *you're* the King of Fire," she snapped.

"You got us into this mess in the first place. Figure something out, great King."

She was making fun of me! I got angry.

"Fine," I said. I waved my knife over my head. "The first thing I'll do as King is to make this forest light up so we can see where we're going! Obey me, forest!" I shouted. *"Obey me!"*

Nothing happened of course, and I stopped waving the knife.

"See?" I snapped at Erin. "Some King of Fire I am, huh? I can't even—"

I stopped talking.

Erin gasped, and threw her hand up over her mouth.

"Wow," Bobby whispered.

We froze. We didn't breathe. Because all around us, the forest was beginning to grow lighter, and lighter, and lighter.

16

All around us, the forest grew brighter. Not the entire forest . . . only around *us*. It was wild! It was like a giant beam of light had come out of the sky, brightening the area where we were standing. I could see trees and branches. I could see Erin and Bobby, and I could see the cracked roots where the raccoon had disappeared. The light was all around us. It was really freaky. The rest of the forest was dark, but the area around us was lit up like daylight!

"I don't suppose this means that you'll bow at my feet and worship me as your king, huh?" I asked Erin quietly.

She shook her head and rolled her eyes. "Fat chance of that. But—how did you do this?" She waved her arm around in front of her. "How did you make this light appear?"

"I don't know," I said. I looked at my knife. Maybe it had some kind of mystical powers, after all. It sure was cool looking.

We just stood there for a moment, looking around us. The light seemed to come out of nowhere. The trees, the brush, the ground below us, all seemed to glow on their own. It was very strange.

"Well, now what?" Erin asked again, and again I shook my head. Now that we could see, I wasn't sure if we should try and find our way out of the forest or not. I certainly didn't want to be in any war fighting weird spirits!

Besides, if we started walking, we might be out of the light in just a few short steps. Then we'd be in darkness again, and just as lost as ever. At the moment, we were still lost . . . but at least we could see around a little bit.

I was about to speak when I heard a noise. I turned my head, listening. It was that same sound we'd heard when the spirits were flying overhead. The sound of hissing wind.

"THERE THEY ARE!" a gruff voice suddenly boomed from the sky. When I looked up, I knew instantly that we were in deep trouble.

17

Above us, just above the treetops, was a spirit.

An *ugly* one.

It had huge ears and big claws for hands. A pointed chin and a wide, v-shaped mouth. Two huge eyes glared down at us. The creature seemed to be floating in the air, without the aid of wings or anything to hold it up.

And it was coming toward us.

"THEY'RE HERE!" the spirit shouted. "RIGHT HERE!"

Erin grabbed Bobby and tried to hide behind a tree trunk. "Do something!" she hissed. "Do something quick!"

"Like what?!?!?" I shouted back. I was terrified. How would we get away from this thing? It was enormous . . . as big as a car!

I looked around. There was nowhere to run. We were trapped. I was sure we were about to be devoured by awful spirits.

The only place to hide was the crack in the root system at the bottom of a tree — the same place where the raccoon had hidden. But the opening was far too small for any of us to fit through.

Suddenly, the raccoon's wispy white face appeared between the roots! Let me tell you, I still was not used to seeing the spirit of a raccoon. Especially up close! His misty-white nose twitched as he spoke.

"Use your knife!" the raccoon whispered. "Use it to make the hole bigger! Then you can climb in here!"

Huh? Not only was he a raccoon spirit, he was a *crazy* raccoon spirit! How could I make the opening wider with my knife?!?! There was no way I would have the time to carve out a hole big enough to fit through!

But I had to do something. The creature above us was coming closer and closer by the second. I was afraid that in just a few more seconds, not only would he be upon us . . . but there might be hundreds of other creatures with him as well!

But maybe we had a chance, after all. I had

created that light a few moments ago, hadn't I? I knew that the knife had some kind of special powers, but I guess I just wasn't really sure how to use it.

Without thinking a second longer, I placed the blade of the knife between the split roots and pulled.

I heard splitting wood. The blade was suddenly buried in the tree trunk, and I struggled to pull it upward.

It was moving! The blade was actually *slicing* the tree trunk! There was no way that I was strong enough to split open a root that size, but I was doing it! It had to be the knife!

Erin peeked her head around the corner to see what I was doing, and her jaw dropped. I continued struggling with the knife.

"I . . . I think . . . I can . . . get . . . this . . . open far enough . . . to –"

"KEVIN!" Erin shouted. *"Look out!"*

I turned and rolled to the ground, pulling the knife blade from the tree.

The spirit-creature. It was almost on top of me! And what was worse, there was another one just above him! They were attacking!

But I had my knife. I knew that somehow,

someway, my knife was very powerful.

After I rolled a couple of times, I knelt on my knees. I slashed my knife up into the air, waving it at the spirit.

He backed away!

His head snapped back, and he drew back. He was afraid!

But I didn't think he would be afraid for too long. Other spirits were coming now, and it wouldn't be long before we were surrounded.

"Erin! Bobby!" I shouted. *"I think the roots are split far enough apart for you to get inside! Hurry!"*

Erin grabbed Bobby and burst out from behind the tree while I waved my silvery knife at the creatures in the air above us. They were keeping their distance . . . at least for now.

Erin grabbed the two roots and began to pull, exposing a dark, gaping hole in the ground.

"Go!" she shouted to Bobby.

"I'm afraid!" Bobby screamed.

"There's no time to be afraid!" she yelled back, and with that, she grabbed Bobby by the shoulders and shoved him between the roots. She looked at me.

"Go!" I yelled to her. *"I'll hold them off! Go now, before it's too late!"*

Erin grabbed the roots and wriggled herself between them.

She was gone. She was gone, and safe . . . hopefully.

But I still had to get away. The spirit-creatures above me were getting closer. It was obvious that they didn't like the knife, but there was no way I could fight all of them, and they knew it.

Without wasting another second, I rolled to the tree trunk and placed my feet in the hole. I could hear the creatures above me, hissing and spitting in anger. I knew they were almost upon me.

Without looking back over my shoulder, I wriggled between the roots. Dirt fell into my hair and I closed my eyes, hoping that I would make it in time.

"Almost!" I heard Erin shout from the dark opening below me. Then she grabbed my legs and pulled. Loose dirt fell all around me and she pulled harder and harder.

Suddenly, I felt myself falling. I tumbled down and fell to the ground.

I made it! And just in time, too. As I looked out between the split roots, I could see the creatures drifting angrily outside. They were swarming like mad bees now, and there must have been dozens of

them.   I thought it was the craziest site in the
world — until I turned around and saw where I was.

What I saw was too much to believe.

We were in a cave of sorts. The floor of the cave was dirt, the walls were dirt, but the ceiling was nothing but an entanglement of roots . . . *roots that glowed like light bulbs!* Each long, spiny root interwove with other roots.

And they each glowed different colors! Some were yellow, some were orange. Still some were kind of pink-ish, and others were green. They looked like thousands of odd-shaped neon tubes that grew from the ceiling. Some hung down, tapering off to a fine point. It was the most bizarre sight I had ever seen — and I had seen quite a few bizarre things lately.

Erin and Bobby were standing in front of me, staring up at the strange root system. Behind us, I could hear the strange spirit-creatures just beyond the tree, trying to get in. The crack in the roots wasn't big enough for them, and I sure was glad about that.

"Where are we?" Erin asked.

"Underground, I guess," I answered.

Erin turned around. "Like, duh," she sneered. "But I've never seen anything like this before. Roots aren't supposed to glow."

"Actually, they are," I said, recalling a part of my outdoor survival handbook. "It's called foxfire. Some roots will glow if their bark is stripped from them."

"Like this?" Erin said, pointing to the mass of roots above us. They glowed so brightly that it was like being in daylight.

"Well, at least we can see where we are," I reasoned. "We won't be stumbling around in the dark anymore."

"But where does this cave go to?" Erin asked. She took a few steps forward. Bobby reached out and grabbed her hand and followed behind her.

I looked back up at the glowing roots above our head. The 'ceiling' was only a few inches above my head, and I slowly reached up and touched a root. It felt smooth and maybe even a bit warm. I pulled on it, and some clumps of dirt fell away.

This was so strange. First, a face in the smoke. Then the odd 'spirit' animals, and the horrible spirits that flew across the treetops looking for us.

And now, a cave with glowing roots! This was too much.

Erin was on the other side of the cave when all of a sudden she crouched low to the ground, followed by Bobby.

"Kevin!" she whispered loudly. *"You're not going to believe this! Come quick!"*

19

I walked quickly to where Erin and Bobby were kneeling on the ground. It looked like they were peering though a hole of some sort.

"What?" I whispered, dropping to my knees. Erin pointed to what appeared to be a window in the wall. It was a round hole, big enough to crawl through. Glowing roots dangled over the hole like neon drapes, but I could clearly see what was on the other side of them.

Moles.

Not just any moles . . . but HUGE moles! Moles that were as big as I was!

Now, if you've never seen a mole before, they are *usually* about the size of a chipmunk. They're dark gray, and they have long, sharp claws for burrowing through the earth. They have tails, but there's no fur on them.

But these moles were like industrial-sized moles! Their claws were bigger than my hands. Their fur was a velvety-gray, and their tails were about four feet long.

I didn't know what to do. I don't think they had spotted us, because they were busy burrowing into the dirt, making a tunnel.

And they worked fast! In just a few seconds, the moles had almost disappeared. They had burrowed into the ground, continuing on their way.

The three of us could only watch as the over-sized moles disappeared in the large holes they had created.

Bobby was excited.

"I want one!" he exclaimed, trying to pull away from Erin's tight grip. "I want one for a pet!"

Sheesh. That's my brother for you.

"I never knew that any place like this existed," Erin said, looking around the strange cave. "It's too weird."

"You can say that again," I said. I turned and looked back at the cracked roots where we had come in. The strange spirit-creatures appeared to be gone, and I could only see darkness through the opening.

We were safe . . . at least for the time being.

Looking around, I found a passage that seemed to lead off into another direction.

"Stay here," I said to Erin and Bobby. Erin shot me a nasty look.

"I don't think so," she said, shaking her head. "From now, on, we're staying together." She looked up at the roots, and then around the cave. "It'll be too easy to get lost."

I walked toward the tunnel that lead deeper underground. Erin and Bobby followed closely behind.

It was at this point that I began to really wonder how all of this was happening. First we get lost looking for a six-toed bear . . . then the strange scene in the fire and smoke . . . followed by animal spirits and then other spirits that I can't even describe.

And my knife.

I still gripped it tightly in my hand, and now I held it up and looked at it. It still shined like new, but it looked ancient and old. It looked powerful and valuable. It looked cool.

"I wonder how that happened?" Erin whispered from behind me, gazing at my knife. "How did your pocket knife change into *that?*"

"Beats me," I answered. "But there's

something really odd about it. I noticed it when I used it to tear the roots away so we could climb down here. It was like the knife did most of the work. I hardly had to do a thing."

I stopped at the mouth of the tunnel. It was like a crude underground subway. Where it went, I could only guess—but I was sure that the moles had created it.

"Look!" Bobby suddenly blurted out. I lowered the knife and looked around the glowing cave. I didn't know what Bobby was talking about—at first.

Then, the air directly in front of me seemed to change. In front of us, just a few feet away, a strange mist was forming. It was swirling and dancing before us, and I took a step back and bumped into Erin, who bumped into Bobby, who fell down.

"Hey!" he squealed, scrambling to his feet. "Watch where you guys are going!"

But Erin and I weren't listening. We were focused on the strange, swirling mist that was growing right in front of us.

And it didn't take long to figure out what it was.

20

I took another step back, holding out my knife like a warrior. The mist kept swirling and swirling, faster and faster, and I began to make out features.

It was a face. Not just a face, but the same face that had formed over the fire!

The old Indian!

I could clearly recognize him now. It was only his head and face, no body, and it was bigger than I was! I sure felt small, standing there in the glowing tunnel, my eyes glued to the bizarre sight in front of me.

Erin was behind me and she grabbed my arm. Bobby ducked for cover, grabbing Erin's leg and trying to hide behind it. A hand flew up over his face and he tried to peek between his two fingers, quickly closing them when he saw the face, only to re-open his fingers again to sneak another peak. If I hadn't been so scared, I would've thought Bobby looked pretty funny!

But it wasn't funny. I couldn't tell if the old Indian was mean or not. He had a grim look on his face, like he was angry.

But there was also something sad about his face, too. I couldn't quite figure it out. Was he angry . . . or sad?

The Indian . . . or at least, the misty face in front of us . . . slowly opened his mouth to speak.

"So," he began quietly. His voice was deep and booming, but at the same time soft. Even gentle. I relaxed a little bit, but I still clung tightly to my knife. "You *are* the one," he continued. "You are the one after all. It was written that you would return."

I'd had about enough. Sure, I was a bit frightened . . . but all that stuff about the 'King of Fire' was getting on my nerves.

"All right," I interrupted the strange misty face. "Just who do you think I am?"

The old face paused a moment, then spoke. His voice was patient and gentle. He smiled.

"Many, many years ago, the great Indian warrior North Bear was the mightiest protector of the forest. When the wicked spirits tried to take over, it was North Bear who led our warriors into battle." The old Indian's voice rumbled through the cavern like an earthquake. "The fighting was fierce, and many souls were lost, but North Bear and his army of forest spirits succeeded in repelling the wicked spirits. But, he knew that when they grew strong again, they would return. They would return to take over the Realm of the Underforest."

"What is the 'Realm of the Underforest'?" I asked.

The old Indian seemed to smile. "The Realm of the Underforest is an ancient world that exists beneath the world that you come from. It is a land all of its own. In many ways, it is like your world. However, in many ways, it is very different."

"I'll say," Erin said. "We don't have giant moles and weird smokey creatures in our world."

The old Indian's face grew very serious.

"Yes, you do," he said gravely. "Avan-Dar and his army want to take over the Realm of the Underforest. If he succeeds, he will not stop. He will not stop until he has conquered *your* world."

I felt Erin's hand tighten on my arm. When I looked down, Bobby was crouched on the ground, both hands over his eyes, his fingers spread apart, peering at the strange sight. The old Indian continued.

"Many, many years ago, North Bear called upon all of the powers of the earth and sky, casting a spell into the future. When the wicked spirits grew strong enough to attack once again, North Bear vowed to return. When he returned, he would be known as the King of Fire, and he will lead the spirits of the forest to victory, once and for all, over the terrible powers of the dark spirits."

I know it might sound funny, but I almost started laughing! I mean . . . come on! This was something out of a movie or a comic book.

"I think you've got the wrong guy if you think that I'm your 'King of Fire'," I said, laughing. "My name is Kevin Barnes. Sure, I'm from the south . . . about four hundred miles, actually. But I'm no 'King of Fire'."

The old Indian smiled a calm, easy grin, and spoke.

"Hold out your knife."

"Huh?"

"Do as I say."

I hesitated for a moment, then I held out my knife.

"Now . . . let go of it."

94

"You . . . you mean, like . . . drop it?"

"Yes," the huge face commanded.

I released my grip on the knife, and pulled my hand away.

The knife remained in the air, perfectly still! I gasped, and I could hear Erin do the same over my shoulder.

All of a sudden the knife began to float—very slowly—back to my hand! Within seconds, the handle was at my palm! It was as if it was trying to get back to my hand! It was incredible.

"So you see," the old Indian said, smiling. "You *are* the chosen one. You are the King of Fire. You will lead the spirits of the forest into battle."

I was in a state of shock. Seeing the knife just kind of 'sit' in the air and float back to my hand was too much.

So I tried it again. This time, I gave it a little push, as if I was tossing it aside.

The knife drifted a few feet away, stopped in mid-air, and gently came right back to my hand.

"Your knife will never leave you," the old Indian said, "unless you choose to give it away. It is the very knife used by North Bear. It is very powerful, and you must use it wisely. But do not *ever* give it away."

"Use it?" I asked. "What for? I've only used a knife to whittle sticks. What am I supposed to use it for?"

The face of the Indian grew grim, and he began to fade. The mist started to drift off, but he spoke.

"You will need to use it now, I'm afraid. The battle has begun. Stay strong . . . and remember — if you use the knife wisely, you will win. You *must* win. To save the Realm of the Underforest . . . and your own world . . . you *must* win."

And with that, the old Indian faded. The old Indian faded, but what we didn't know was that behind us, another mist was forming in the cave.

Avan-Dar had returned.

21

I didn't even see him until I heard his voice. After hearing the way he spoke at the campfire, I would recognize *that* voice anywhere. It was a terrible hissing voice, like a lizard with a bad cold and a sore throat.

Avan-Dar. His mouth moved, and he began to speak.

"You think you will win, do you?" he said in his terrible, throaty wheeze. "Well, think again, young one, think again. You are no match for me. I have been alive for thousands and thousands of years. I am strong and powerful. Now . . . if you give me that knife, I just might let you leave this forest. I might even be so kind to take you back to your campsite . . . where your mother and father are."

His face was twisted and distorted, and the mist kept swirling. His features kept changing, and it never looked the same for more than a few seconds.

And I knew he was lying to me. I knew there was no way he'd take us back to Mom and Dad.

"You're not having my knife," I said boldly. "It stays with me."

"Oh, but it is your only hope," Avan-Dar said in his raspy, arrogant tone. "There is only one way that you can leave the Realm of the Underforest unharmed," Avan-Dar taunted. "You must simply take my hand. Take my hand, and place the knife in my palm."

In the next instant, the mist that Avan-Dar was made of formed a weird, cane-like arm, with bony fingers at the end. The fingers wriggled and curled, and tiny wisps of smoke broke away and dwindled off. As Avan-Dar reached out toward me, I backed away.

"There, there," the spirit coaxed. "There's nothing to be afraid of. Just hand the knife . . . *to me.*"

The swirling, misty white hand waved in front of me, reaching for the knife.

"Don't let him have it," Erin whispered.

"*I'm not going to,*" I whispered back.

"Oh, yes you will," the wicked Avan-Dar hissed.

Suddenly, his hazy arm grabbed mine! It felt like a vice had hold of my wrist! I know that Avan-Dar seemed like he was made out of smoke . . . but he sure was strong!

"Let me go!" I shouted. "Let me go!" I tried to squirm and wriggle free, but it was no use. He was crushing my arm! The pain was terrible.

"Give me that knife," Avan-Dar hissed again. "Give it to me now, and I'll let you live. All of you."

"*No!*" I screamed back in anger. "*I WILL NOT GIVE IT TO YOU! I AM THE KING OF FIRE!*"

Avan-Dar froze. His grip loosened. Time seemed to stop.

All of a sudden a blinding-white flame shot from the knife in my hand! It glowed bright and strong, spreading about in the air before me. It surprised me as much as Avan-Dar. Even Erin and Bobby jumped back, afraid of what might happen next.

But I was angry. I was angry, and I knew that my knife held *power.*

I swept it back and forth toward Avan-Dar, and his misty form retreated, backing away from the intense fire. Oddly, I didn't feel any heat myself, even though the fire was only inches from my hand. The flame shot out a few feet like a glowing white sword.

I swept it back and forth a couple times and took a step toward Avan-Dar.

He retreated even farther! He was afraid! Avan-Dar was really afraid!

"Leave us alone," I commanded. "Leave us alone right now."

"You don't know what you're doing," Avan-Dar hissed. His face was twisted and ugly and mean, but I could tell that he was afraid of me. Or afraid of the knife, at least.

I took another step toward him, and he took another step back. I turned around and shot a glance behind me to make sure that Erin and Bobby were all right. Bobby was hiding behind Erin, both hands over his eyes. His fingers were spread and he was peeking between them.

I turned back around quickly to confront Avan-Dar.

"Leave us!" I commanded. "Leave us now!"

"This is not the end," Avan-Dar hissed menacingly. "This is only the beginning!"

And with that, the mist Avan-Dar was made

of began to seep into the dirt wall of the cave! It swirled and swished for a moment, and suddenly Avan-Dar was gone. I was facing only a wall of dirt.

The flame that shot out of my knife began to shorten and fade, and in seconds it was completely gone. I touched the blade.

It was cold! I was sure that the blade would have been hot from the fire, but the blade was cold!

This was very strange.

But it was about to get a lot stranger.

22

There was something else coming out of the dirt wall in front of me. I was sure of it. I could hear something in the ground, making noise. It sounded like a dull scraping. I stepped back to where Bobby and Erin stood.

"What is it?" Erin asked. She could hear it, too.

"I . . . I don't know," I stammered.

The noise grew louder. It sounded like a bulldozer . . . an underground bulldozer, plowing through the wall.

Suddenly, dirt began to fall away from the wall before us. Small pieces of glowing root began to fall to the ground. Whatever it was, it was coming into the cave!

We couldn't step back any farther, as we were

already backed up against the dirt wall of the cave. Stringy, glowing roots tangled in my hair, but I didn't really notice. I was too fascinated—and maybe a little bit scared—of whatever it was that was burrowing through the ground. I held my knife out in front of me, ready for action.

And then I knew. I knew what it was, because there was only one thing that could move through the ground like that. And we'd already seen them only a short time ago.

Giant moles.

All of a sudden the wall crumbled right before our eyes! Large chunks of dirt fell to the ground, and a large hole was exposed.

And there was movement in the hole. I couldn't tell what it was for sure, but I was certain that it had to be one of the super huge moles that we'd seen when we first entered the strange underground cavern.

Behind me, Erin stood rigid and frozen. Bobby still held his hands over his eyes, peeking through his fingers.

And then we saw them. They came through the holes easily. Two of them.

Giant moles.

They stopped moving and sat hunched in the

other side of the cave, looking at us. Their tiny black eyes just stared at us, and we stared back. I held out my knife so they could see it. I hoped that maybe they would be afraid.

But who was I kidding? They were *moles.* Actual moles that dug tunnels in the ground . . . except they were about a hundred times bigger than normal moles. Most moles would fit in the palm of my hand. These moles were as big as we were! Why would they be afraid of a kid with a knife?

But I'm not just a kid anymore, I thought. *I'm the King of Fire. I have special powers.*

Then one mole turned to the other mole.

"It's him," I heard the mole whisper.

He talked! He actually *spoke!* This was the most bizarre camping trip I had ever been on. Spirits, glowing roots, talking moles . . . it was like something out of a movie.

Both of the moles were looking at me now.

"You . . . you can talk?" I asked the moles.

The creatures were silent for a moment, and then one spoke.

"Of course we can," one of them said. "But we don't have time to talk now. You must come with us. Quickly."

"What do you mean?" I responded. "Go

where?"

"We have made tunnels beneath the forest," the other mole said, motioning with a pink, bone-like paw to the hole behind them. "You'll be safe if you follow us."

I still wasn't sure about all of this. How was I supposed to know if the moles were actually friendly? Maybe they were luring us into a trap.

Suddenly I felt something on my neck, and I reached up to swipe it away. My hand felt something long and stiff, about the width of a pencil. It scratched my skin as it rolled down the side of my neck. I slapped at it . . . but then it started moving faster!

I jumped back, swatting at whatever was crawling around my neck. It felt like it was trying to wrap itself around me!

I looked up, and what I saw made me gasp in horror.

The glowing roots that were dangling from above were moving! They were slithering about like snakes, growing longer by the second, reaching for us! All around and above, long thin tentacles were reaching out like wiry fingers, reaching, reaching, *reaching* . . . .

23

I knew right then that it would be impossible to escape. Oh, how I wished I wouldn't have followed those bear tracks away from camp! I wished that we were all around the campfire, singing songs and eating toasted marshmallows.

Erin screamed as a green root swooped from above, slithering toward her in the air. She ducked sideways and got out of its way, but the root snapped around . . . *and grabbed Bobby!*

Bobby started screaming his head off. The long, green root slipped around his waist, pulling him into the air. He grabbed at the root that tightened around his waist, but it was no use. The root had taken on a life of its own, and now had Bobby in its grasp.

"It's Avan-Dar!" one of the moles shouted. "His spirit has taken over the roots! You must use your knife! It's your only hope!"

I sprang into action. Holding my knife in front of me, I lunged at the root that had pulled Bobby up into the air. I swung hard, coming down on the root with the sharp, silver blade.

Nothing happened. The knife didn't do anything to the root at all.

Another root shot down and lunged for me and I stepped aside, falling to the ground. I rolled away from the root and stopped. Laying on my back, I could see the horrible sight above me.

All of the glowing roots had come to life! They were swirling above me, swaying to and fro, like a ball of angry snakes, ready to strike. It was the most horrible sight I had ever seen in my life.

All at once a high-pitched scream wailed in my ears.

Erin!

A root had taken hold of her and was pulling her off the ground!

"Use your knife!" both of the moles shouted. "USE YOUR KNIFE!"

A long, blue root shot toward me, stopping just inches from my face. Then it began to grow! In seconds, it was twice the size it had been.

And it began to grow a head and a face, and I knew in an instant what I was staring at. I'd seen them on TV, and once I saw one at the zoo.

I was face to face with one of the deadliest snakes in the world.

A king cobra.

Only this wasn't just any ordinary king cobra. This one was long and blue and had a face that I recognized immediately.

It was a cobra—with the face of Avan-Dar. His head flared wide and he slowly swayed back and forth, to and fro.

"You," he hissed. When he spoke, a red tongue slithered from his mouth, wagging back and forth. He looked angry and mean, and I tried to crawl away, but he followed me. His face was right in front of mine.

"You think you'll win," the snake hissed. "You think that because you've got your knife, you can do anything you want. Well, mister 'King of Fire', you are about to meet your match. Prepare yourself . . . *for the wrath of Avan-Dar!*"

The terrible cobra lurched back, his mouth open, preparing to strike. I could see his two sharp fangs pointing downward like sharp daggers, ready to plunge into my flesh.

"THE KNIFE!! THE KNIFE!!" the moles yelled in unison. "USE YOUR KNIFE!"

But it was too late. The giant blue king cobra lunged.

I rolled sideways and kept rolling, holding my knife above my head so I wouldn't cut myself with the razor-sharp blade. When I glanced to the side, I could see the head of the snake over my shoulder. He had missed me by mere inches!

I thrust my knife in front of me, sweeping it from side to side, aiming for the snake . . . and then the unthinkable happened.

The snake — Avan-Dar — twisted back around . . . and lunged for the knife! He surprised me so much that I almost let go — *almost*. I held the handle firmly and pulled with all my might. The snake held the blade in his mouth, trying to wretch the knife from my hands.

This was madness. I have never felt so helpless in my life. Bobby and Erin were still in the clutches of the awful glowing roots, and I was powerless to do anything. At the moment, I couldn't help them if I tried.

Or . . . maybe I could.

"Fire!" I suddenly blurted out.

Avan-Dar stopped tugging, and a strange look came over his snake-like face. The roots that had been swirling above me with a life of their own suddenly stopped. Erin and Bobby were able to scramble free.

And my knife.

A long flame shot out again, making a glowing white sword. I quickly swung it back, aiming for Avan-Dar . . . and swept the fiery blade toward his head.

Avan-Dar, still looking very much like a blue King Cobra made out of a root, snapped back quickly.

He wasn't fast enough.

The blade came down, severing the root in half! Avan-Dar's head fell to the ground! It was over!

But then again, not quite.

Because as soon as the 'head' hit the floor, it was nothing but a root! It was just a piece of glowing blue root that lay before me on the ground.

Everything was quiet. The roots had stopped their strange wriggling. Nothing more happened.

The two moles still sat in the corner, terrified, watching the crazy scene before them.

"Hurry!" one of them said. "You must follow

us!"

"But we're safe now," I said. "I just got rid of Avan-Dar."

"Only for the moment," the mole answered. "He'll be back. Come . . . you must follow us. You'll be safe."

I turned and looked at Erin. She shrugged and looked back at me. "Anyplace is better than here," she said, glancing up at the tangled, glowing roots above her.

And with that, she took Bobby by the hand, and the three of us hurried after the moles into the long, dark tunnel.

24

Unlike the cavern we had just left, this tunnel was totally dark. No glowing roots, no light, nothing. I pulled my small penlight from my pocket, but the light was very dim. I could barely see the ground we were walking on.

And another strange thing: the moles had vanished! There was no sign of them anywhere. The only thing I could think of was that they can move much faster than we can underground. Maybe they were up ahead of us.

"I wonder where this goes to?" Erin asked.

"I don't know," I answered. "But I wouldn't be surprised if it led to Egypt. This whole night has been really weird."

I led the way as we trudged along, with Erin and Bobby behind me. We walked slowly and quietly, not knowing what we'd gotten ourselves into. Maybe the moles had lured us into a trap, after all. Maybe at this moment, Avan-Dar was waiting to strike, taking the form of another root or something.

Soon, we came to a place where the trail split in two. Before us were two dark tunnels.

"Great," Erin sighed. "We are going to get more lost than ever. We're never going to get out of here if we keep going."

"It's better than being in that cave with all of those glowing roots that attacked us," I answered.

"That wasn't the roots," Erin replied. "That was Avan-Dar. He took over the roots."

Erin was right. I had to remember that. Avan-Dar was dangerous. If he could take over roots and actually become part of the roots himself, what else was he capable of taking over?

We stood, staring at the two tunnels. I had no idea which way to go.

"Eenie, meanie, miney, moe," I said. As I spoke the words, I held my knife out before me, swinging it back and forth, pointing from one tunnel to the next.

Suddenly, the knife began to pull away from me! It was like something was trying to take the knife away from me!

I held tight, not sure what was happening. The knife seemed to be pointing! It was pointing to the tunnel to the left!

And when I tried to point the knife to the tunnel on the right, the knife seemed to struggle and pull back toward the left.

I decided to try an experiment.

Slowly, I released my grip on the handle.

The knife froze in mid-air! It remained motionless in the air, with the blade pointing to the tunnel on the left.

Behind me, Erin gasped.

"Wow!" Bobby exclaimed. "How did you do that?"

"I . . . I don't know," I answered. "I just let go of it."

"Well, I guess we know which direction to take," Erin said matter-of-factly.

I reached out and grasped the knife handle. We set off again, down the tunnel that went to the left. Wherever we were going, I hoped we would get there soon. The batteries in my penlight weren't going to hold out much longer.

As fate would have it, we didn't have to walk much farther. The tunnel suddenly stopped at a big, black door made of wood . . . and there were noises coming from the other side!

25

I drew closer, training the fading beam of my penlight on the huge door. It was easily twice as big as I was. There was a large white handle on the right that appeared to be made out of bone of some sort.

The noises from behind the door were just that—noises. For a moment, I thought I heard someone talking. Then all I heard was some shuffling. Then, more noise like a crowd of people mumbling.

Whatever the sounds were, they were coming from behind the door.

I grasped the door handle and looked up at Erin. Her eyes were filled with fear.

"Wait," she said suddenly. "What if it's where Avan-Dar lives?" she asked.

Good point.

"We have to take the chance," I said finally. "We either open this door or we go back the way we came. And I'm not sure I want to go back and get attacked by glowing roots."

"But what if he is waiting?" Erin insisted. "What if he's waiting for us right behind this door? Him and all of those ugly flying things?"

It wasn't a pleasant thought. We were in way over our heads, and the more I thought about it, the more I started to think that opening the door might not be such a good idea.

But then again, no. We had no other choice. We had to see what was on the other side of the door. Maybe it was a way out. Maybe we would open the door and find ourselves in St. Ignace. Hard to believe, but right now, I thought just about anything was possible.

I looked at Bobby. He had covered his face again, and was peering out between split fingers. I looked at Erin.

"We're going in," I stated confidently.

Erin nodded slowly. "I guess you're right," she said. "We really don't have much of a choice."

I reached out and grasped the door handle. *Here goes nothing,* I thought.

I pulled on the door handle.

Nothing happened. The huge door wouldn't budge! I twisted and turned the handle, but it was frozen solid. The door wouldn't open.

I could still hear noises coming from the other side, and I debated whether or not if I should pound on the door. Maybe someone from the other side could let us in.

But, then again, if it was Avan-Dar's army, we'd really be in trouble!

I was staring at the door, wondering what to do next. Bobby started to pull on my pant leg.

"Knock it off," I said, not looking at him, but he continued to pull on my pant leg. "Hey!" I scolded. "Cool it, will ya?" I turned to glance down at him.

He wasn't looking at me. He was looking the other way, back down the tunnel we had just came from.

And out of the corner of my eye, I saw a movement. Erin turned, and we both saw it at the same time.

An earthworm.

Not just any earthworm—but an enormous, super-sized earthworm! His whole body filled the tunnel.

But what was worse, the earthworm had a face. It was all snarled and angry, full of hatred and fury.

It was the face of Avan-Dar.

26

At that moment, every single hair on my body stood up. A chill ran all the way down my spine and down my legs. Erin's hand flew up to her mouth to muffle her scream. Bobby just kept pointing, wagging his finger back and forth at the giant, slimy worm that was crawling toward us in the tunnel.

And the face.

It was a sneering, snarling face. A face of anger and fury.

The face of Avan-Dar.

Another chill ran down my spine, and I could feel every single hair on my body stand on end. Erin drew a hand to her mouth to muffle a scream. Bobby just kept pointing at the huge, grotesque form coming our way.

Avan-Dar made no sound, except for his

squishy sounds of his shiny, wet body slithering through the tunnel.

I backed up against the door. Erin backed up next to me, and she grabbed Bobby and held him close.

And Avan-Dar kept coming toward us.

It's hard to imagine a giant worm in the first place—but try to imagine a giant worm with the ugliest face in the world!

A face that was coming closer and closer by the second.

"Do something!" Erin whispered loudly. *"Use your knife or something."*

Good idea!

But there was one problem. When I pulled my knife out and pointed it at Avan-Dar, it wasn't a knife anymore! It was—

A KEY!

The knife had changed into a big skeleton key! How was I going to fight off Avan-Dar with a key?!?!

Okay . . . sometimes I can be a bit slow at figuring things out . . . but not this time!

I spun around, pointing the key at the door. I knew that there was a keyhole in the door somewhere.

There had to be.

"What are you doing?!?!?" Erin hissed, her voice trembling with fear. "He's getting closer!"

"This key opens the door!" I replied anxiously. "It has to!"

"Hurry up! Hurry up!" Erin shouted. "He's almost here!"

Bobby started to cry. Out of the corner of my eye, I could make out the huge form of Avan-Dar—the giant worm—coming closer and closer.

And then my knife—I mean, the key—found the keyhole! It slipped in so easily that I was surprised that I hadn't noticed it before. The entire key seemed to just disappear within the door!

"Hurry!" Erin pleaded.

"I am, I am!" I shouted.

I turned the key.

It worked! As the key turned in the keyhole, I heard a few loud clinks as the tumblers turned. Then there was a loud, solid *thunk!* . . . and I knew the door would open.

At least, I *hoped* it would open! I pulled the door handle, and suddenly, almost magically, the door squeaked open. Without even looking, I shoved Erin and Bobby through the opening. I glanced back to see the huge earthworm only a few feet from me. Avan-Dar's face was gargantuan, and I couldn't believe that he could change into so many different things.

Too weird.

Without wasting another precious second, I pulled the large key from the keyhole, flew threw the open door, and pulled it closed behind me.

Whew! That was a close one.

"I think we made it," I said to Erin and Bobby, breathing a sigh of relief.

"Not so fast," Erin stammered. I could tell from her voice that something was wrong, and it was then that I turned away from the door and looked to see where we were.

Holy cow!

27

There were only two words that came to mind that could describe the place that we were now in: totally bizarre.

They were everywhere. Spirits, that is. Hundreds of them. Maybe thousands. They looked like the spirits that we had seen in the forest, by the campfire. Strange, wispy, animal-like spirits.

And they were all looking at us!

There didn't seem to be any ground or floor, just a smokey, gray mist that drifted like thick carpeting.

And there wasn't any sky, either. Above us was nothing but black. Yet, there was a strange glow coming from somewhere that seemed to give off light. It wasn't like a sun or anything, just an eerie glow.

I'm not sure how long the three of us stood there—Erin, Bobby, and I—just watching the hundreds of spirits watching us. They seemed to float in the air without the aid of any legs or anything. But—

So did we!

When I looked down, I saw that we, too, seemed to just drift above the strange, gray mist beneath us. It was a bit unnerving at first, and I had the sensation that I might fall at any second, plunging through the gray into who knows where.

But it didn't happen. Wherever we were, I figured we were probably safer here than on the other side of that door! I sure didn't want to do battle with Avan-Dar the giant earthworm!

One of the spirits began to drift toward us, and I backed up a little bit. I didn't think he was going to hurt us, but I wasn't sure. As the strange creature floated to meet us, I noticed that many of the other spirits seemed to disappear. They simply were melting into the darkness.

"It is good to have you here, great King," the creature said, bowing his head toward me.

It still felt funny being called a 'king'.

"Just where are we?" Erin asked, looking around. By now, most of the other spirits had simply vanished into thin air.

"This is the Realm of the UnderForest," the creature replied, coming closer still. "This is our home. This is where all of the spirits of the forest live."

Now, about the creature that was drifting toward us.

He was big, maybe about the size of a bear. And he looked like a bear, except for a few odd features. His nose was bigger than a bear's nose, and his ears were, too. And he seemed much more agile and sleek than a bear. He looked like he might be a cross between a bear and some other animal. I didn't ask him.

"Where did all of the other . . . uh, creatures go?" I asked.

"They've gone to prepare for battle, of course," the spirit answered. "We'll meet up with them shortly. We will meet up with them when we are ready to fight Avan-Dar's army."

"Now hang on a minute," I said. "We've got to figure a few things out. First off, how are we going to fight Avan-Dar's army? And how are we—my brother and sister and I—going to make it back to camp where Mom and Dad are?"

"I don't know where that is," the creature

replied. "But I can tell you how we're going to do battle with Avan-Dar."

Now we were getting somewhere.

"We will leave the Realm of the UnderForest soon," the creature began. "Using your knife, you will cast a wall of white fire around us. This will do two things. First, it will protect us from Avan-Dar and his terrible creatures. But secondly, and most importantly, you will order the wall of fire to become an enormous blanket that will circle Avan-Dar's men. It will cover them up and they won't be able to escape. Avan-Dar's entire army of madness will be devoured in the wall of fire."

If we hadn't already been through what we had, I probably would have laughed. This whole thing seemed so ridiculous . . . and simple! I was going to defeat an entire army of spirits by using my pocket knife . . . which, of course, wasn't a pocket knife anymore. I glanced down at the silvery tool in may hand. It was no longer a key like it had been a few moments ago. It had changed back to a knife.

"Well," Erin said, "if that's all there is to it, then why do you need us? Why can't you do this yourself?"

There was a moment of silence as the spirit-creature looked at Erin, then at me, then at Bobby, than back at me.

"You must stay here," he finally said. "You are the King of Fire. You have been sent here to do battle with Avan-Dar. Only you can help us stop him."

Say what?!?!?!?

But any more questions were going to have to wait, because a strange rumble suddenly rolled through the Realm of the Underforest. Then another spirit appeared out of nowhere.

"Hurry!" it shouted. "We are out of time! Avan-Dar and his army of spirits are attacking! They're trying to take over the Realm of the Underforest!"

28

"Let's go! Now!"

I'm not even sure who said those words, but all of a sudden we were running. I held Erin's hand and she grabbed Bobby and we sprang, following the creature through the strange, dark realm. I had the odd sensation of running on something soft, like jelly. Or maybe a giant sponge. It was really weird, but we were able to run without any problem.

"Where are we going now?!?!?" I shouted.

"We will leave this realm and return to the forest!" the creature answered.

All around us, the rumbling continued. It grew louder and louder. There were strange noises all around, above and below. It seemed like the whole earth was trembling.

And it grew darker! The farther we ran, the

darker it became. Soon, I couldn't even see my feet anymore. I could just barely see the odd creature running in front of us, and it was all we could do to keep up with him.

"*Get ready!*" he suddenly shouted, and without warning, we were thrust into a blinding white light! I threw up my hands to shield my eyes. Then the light flickered and flashed brightly, and we were in darkness once again.

But it was much more than that. We were back in the forest! We were in the forest at night time, but we had entered a battlefield! All around us—in the trees, in the air, everywhere—were ugly, hideous creatures! They were drifting about, their mouths open, their tongues lashing from side to side.

Many of the creatures that I had recognized from the Realm of the Underforest were there, too. They were trying to hold off the larger, more powerful spirits that belonged to Avan-Dar's army.

And they weren't having much luck.

"Use your knife!" I heard a voice shout. "Sweep it around through the air and concentrate! Concentrate on a blanket of fire! Hurry, before it's too late!"

I had no clue what I was doing, but I did it

anyway. Erin crouched low to the ground, holding Bobby tightly while I thrust the knife into the air.

I closed my eyes tightly.

Blanket of fire, I thought. *Blanket of fire. Blanket of Fire. Blanket of —*

"KEVIN!" I heard Erin scream. "WATCH OUT!"

29

Alarmed by Erin's shout, I opened my eyes and got the shock of my life.

Fire!

It was all around us. It was a wall of fire, in the sky, around trees. Everywhere I looked, there was fire. Flames were whirling high into the night sky. There was a thick stream of fire that seemed to shoot out of my knife like water.

But, oddly enough, I couldn't feel any heat! The fire was very close, but I didn't feel it at all.

"You're doing it!" a voice shouted. "It's working! You're doing it! Keep concentrating!"

I closed my eyes tightly, still holding the long knife high above my head. I could feel the power of the fire as it raced upward and around.

Soon, I began to hear screaming. I opened

my eyes to find that the enormous wall of fire had wrapped itself into a ball! The stream of flames was no longer coming from my knife—and all of Avan-Dar's creatures were gone! They were trapped in the ball of fire that was now rising higher and higher into the night sky! I could hear them screaming in anger as the ball of fire held them captive.

All at once a bright explosion lit up the sky like the sun. I dropped to my knees and shielded my eyes. Bobby screamed and Erin gasped.

The light faded to an orange ball. Smoke filled the sky, lit up by the orange glow. The ball of fire continued to fade, darker, darker still.

Gone.

My eyes scanned the sky, searching for any evidence of Avan-Dar's army.

Nothing. They were gone.

I looked around the dark forest. Eyes began to pop up here and there, from behind trees and around bushes. I began to see the shapes of the forest spirits as they came out from their hiding places. Apparently, the ball of fire had scared them, too!

"You did it!" Erin cried, giving me a big hug. Erin doesn't hug me a lot, and I guess this time I didn't really mind it. I was just glad to be alive!

I stood up and pulled Erin up with me. Bobby still sat on the ground, but now, he reluctantly got to his feet.

The swarm of forest spirits gathered around us.

"You did it!" they cried. "Hail to the King of Fire! Hail to the King!"

Boy, did I feel proud. I had saved the forest spirits from Avan-Dar's terrible army.

But I had forgotten one important detail.

Avan-Dar himself.

His army was destroyed, but he was still alive. He was still in the forest, roaming about, probably angrier than ever.

And it was up to me to finish him off. Me and me alone.

I think that the forest spirits had forgotten this fact, too, because they were too busy chattering to see the gigantic figure that was now looming over the dark treetops, waiting to strike.

Avan-Dar.

Suddenly, one of the spirits of the forest cried out.

"Oh no! It's HIM!" A hushed silence fell over the crowd of spirits. All eyes gazed upward, toward the sky. The night became very still and quiet, and very eerie.

And I could *feel* him.

I could feel Avan-Dar watching us, waiting to lash out and strike. Waiting for the moment to devour us all.

"RUN!" one of the spirits shouted. "Back to the Realm of the Underforest!"

The spirits began whirling around us, scurrying off in all directions.

I grabbed Erin's hand, she grabbed Bobby, and we tried to follow — but we were stopped by one of the spirits!

"Where are you going?!?!?!" the spirit asked excitedly.

"Well . . . we're following you guys," I answered. I could hear loud footsteps begin to thrash through the forest. I knew that Avan-Dar was getting closer.

"You must stay and fight!" the spirit-creature told me. "You must stay and fight Avan-Dar! That is what you are here for!"

"But . . . but . . . " I stammered. Suddenly, the creature took flight and was gone. *All* of the spirit-creatures were gone.

There was just me, Erin, and Bobby left.

And Avan-Dar. The terrible, terrible spirit

that inspired so much fear in the forest creatures. I could hear something big trampling through the dark forest.

Closer . . . .

Avan-Dar.

Closer . . . .

And then I could see him. As the huge form began to take shape through the branches, I thought I was going to faint.

30

Nothing I could have imagined would have prepared me for what I was about to see.

It was Avan-Dar, taking the form of some weird dragon. He had sharp spines running down his back, and huge, thick wings. His tail was long, and it thrashed back and forth in the light of the moon. His face was the most hideous thing I had ever seen. An ugly upturned nose. A wide mouth, and red, diamond-shaped eyes.

And he was *big*. He was easily three stories tall. Trees were crushed like brittle twigs beneath his three-clawed feet. The ground shook with every horrible, thundering step.

Okay Kevin, I thought, gripping my knife tightly in my right hand. *Time to take charge.* I kept telling myself this, but it wasn't working very good.

How could I possibly defeat an enemy the size of Avan-Dar? He was big enough to eat a house!

"Get behind those trees!" I shouted to Erin and Bobby. Erin sprang, holding Bobby's hand, and the two of them disappeared into the darkness. I only caught a glimpse of their shadows as they slipped off to hide.

Now it was up to me.

I held my knife firmly, unsure of what to do. I knew my knife was powerful, but I hadn't a clue how to really use it. All I knew was that I could make fire come out of the blade if I really concentrated hard.

So I did. I kept my eyes open, watching the huge, dark form of Avan-Dar come closer and closer.

Come on, I thought, glancing down at the knife blade. *Come on . . . .*

Fire.

Suddenly, a trickle of fire began to form around the blade. It surprised me so much, I almost dropped the knife. It grew longer by the second. The more I concentrated, the longer the flame grew. It was like having a sword — a sword of white fire.

A deep, throaty growl snarled through the forest, shaking leaves from the trees. It was a hideous snarl, a defiant, awful sound.

And Avan-Dar's voice suddenly boomed out through the forest.

"*YOU!*" he wheezed in a gruff, throaty growl that rocked the dark forest like an explosion. "*You will not win this time! This time, you have met your match!*"

At about this time, I was *really* hoping that he was wrong.

But what could I do? I was the size of a bug compared to him. There was no way I could fight Avan-Dar, even with my knife. He towered above the trees. He was like some strange monster out of a *Godzilla* movie.

With every thundering step, he came closer and closer. The ground shook heavily beneath my feet. I've never been in an earthquake before, but I imagined that this would probably be how one would feel.

If only I was bigger, I thought. *If only I was the size of Avan-Dar, then it might be a fair fight.* True, the chance of defeating something his size would be nearly impossible, but right now I was in danger of getting squished!

Avan-Dar's huge head loomed high above me in the darkness, and he looked down. I have never seen such a horrible looking creature in my life.

If only I was bigger, I thought again.

Suddenly, a strange thing began to happen. In a split second, I was looking at a tree top! I felt weird and off balance, like I might fall over. My head seemed to spin, and I felt dizzy.

But I saw the look of amazement on Avan-Dar's face—and I knew instantly what was happening.

31

I was growing. I could feel myself rising upward, above the trees, higher and higher.

And all I had to do was think about it!

In the distance, I could see the lights of St. Ignace. Beyond the city, the lights of Mackinac Island seemed to flicker and blink in the distance.

And Castle Rock! Just north of St. Ignace, right next to the expressway, is an enormous rock cliff that goes way up into the air. I could see the dark pillar of Castle Rock jutting up above the trees.

Avan-Dar was clearly surprised by my newly-found height, but he still was coming toward me.

Okay, I thought. *I want to be TWICE as tall as Avan-Dar!*

That didn't seem to work. I waited for a

moment, hoping to grow taller, but it didn't happen, and I couldn't wait any longer. Avan-Dar had almost reached me.

He lunged forward, and in the bright moonlight I could see his long tongue lashing out. His mouth was open, and his fangs were as big around as some of the trees I was stepping on.

Well, at least I would have a great story to tell my friends at school . . . if I lived that long!

I snapped back and out of the way of Avan-Dar's attack, and I stumbled over a huge pine tree. The tree snapped like a dried twig beneath my feet. My knife and the long blade of fire had grown, too, and as I stumbled I swung the knife to the side. The fire made a deep, loud, *whoooosh!* and it lit up the ground for miles.

Just then I was overcome with a terrible thought:

Where was Erin and Bobby?!?!?

The last I had seen them, they were scurrying away in the darkness! They were right below me somewhere, and if I wasn't careful, I'd step on them!

I scanned the ground, but it was tough to see in the shadows beneath the trees.

Suddenly, Avan-Dar lunged for me again. He was hissing loudly, saying something, but I didn't understand what he said. I dove sideways, in an area that I hoped would be far enough away from Erin and Bobby.

And I fell.

Being so big is kind of clumsy, and I wasn't used to it. As I hit the ground I took out dozens of trees, but I hardly noticed them as they bent and snapped off, crushed beneath my body weight. Besides, I was more focused on keeping my flaming knife away from the trees. I didn't know if it would actually catch the forest on fire, but I wasn't taking any chances!

As I hit the ground, it must have sounded like ten thousand elephants falling.

And it was then that I saw Erin and Bobby.

They were huddled behind a tree, ducking down in the shadows. Both of them were looking at me in disbelief.

Well, Erin was looking at me. Bobby had his hand over his face, and every second or two his fingers would open up and he would peer out between them.

"Stay there!" I whispered loudly. As long as I knew they were safe, I could battle with Avan-Dar and draw his attention away from their hiding spot. I sure didn't want to skoosh my brother and sister!

I leapt to my feet and took a giant step away from Avan-Dar — and away from Erin and Bobby. When I caught my footing I spun, holding out my knife before me. The long pillar of fire stretched upward.

Avan-Dar stopped. I could see his eyes glowing in the firelight. His mouth was open, and he was panting like a dog.

"YOU CANNOT WIN," he hissed, lowering his head. *"YOU CANNOT WIN! "*

I thrust the flaming knife toward him, and he flinched. He backed away, his eyes wide.

He was afraid. He was afraid of the fire.

Again, I thrust the flame toward him, and again, he backed up. This could go on all night.

And then an idea came to me.

That just might work, I thought. It was a daring, risky plan, but I had to try. At the moment, it seemed like my only chance.

32

I glanced down at the fiery beam that extended from the blade of my knife.

Suddenly, the flame began to grow smaller! It was . . . it was going out!

"What's happening?" I asked aloud. The flame dwindled down to a tiny orange spark, flickered a couple of times —

And went out!

"You see!" Avan-Dar hissed in his awful, sneering voice. *"You don't know what you're doing. You do not know how to handle the knife. Now, it is my turn to triumph! I will take over the Realm of the Underforest, and rule forever!"*

And with that, Avan-Dar did an incredible thing.

His wings began to flap. Slowly at first, then

harder.

He was flying! Avan-Dar was hovering above me in the air! I could see his dark shape, blotting out the moon and covering the sky.

And I knew he was getting closer.

"You should have never come here," Avan-Dar hissed. *"You should have never come back."*

I waited. It was the hardest thing I think I've ever had to do.

Wait.

My heart knocked in my chest. My breathing was heavy and full.

And Avan-Dar came closer.

And I waited.

"Prepare yourself!" Avan-Dar growled. "This is the end of you! Until forevermore, I will rule the Realm of the Underforest!" He was now almost directly over me, his mouth open, his terrible tongue swinging back and forth. I could feel his hot and smelly breath on me.

Suddenly, he lunged! He opened his mouth wide and shouted as he struck.

"Prepare yourself! Prepare to—"

I didn't give him time to finish. I thrust my knife upward, directly at Avan-Dar.

"FIRE!" I screamed as loudly as I could.

A thunderous explosion rocked the forest, and a brilliant yellow light shot out from the blade of my knife! A towering swath of fire shot upward, up, up—and right into Avan-Dar.

The fire suddenly closed in around him, forming a blanket that went all around his body. I could hear him screeching and screaming from within the boiling flames. Fire continued to flow from my knife, and I watched as Avan-Dar began to disappear. His screaming grew faint, and as the fire raged on in the sky, it became harder and harder to see Avan-Dar within the tight tongues of flame. The fire faded, grew smaller, and faded some more. There was no sight of Avan-Dar, no sounds from the sky. Soon, the flames were completely gone, except for the pillar of fire coming from my knife.

I stopped concentrating, and the fire from the blade gradually grew smaller and went out. All of a sudden I began to grow smaller, too. I felt myself lowering to the ground, down, down, to the treetops, below the branches and lower still. In moments, I was my own self again.

Bummer. There's a couple of kids at school that used to pick on me. Boy . . . I could have taught them a thing or two if I was three stories tall!

Erin and Bobby came running over.

"Did you see that?!?!?" I exclaimed.

"How could we not see it?" Erin replied as she reached me. "You almost burned down the whole forest!"

Never mind that I had saved the Realm of the Underforest from the wrath of Avan-Dar . . . my sister only complained about starting a forest fire!

We were silent for a moment. This sure was going to be a night I'd never forget.

"How did you do it?" Erin asked. "For a minute, I thought you were a goner!"

"I tricked Avan-Dar into thinking that the fire from my knife blade had gone out," I replied smartly. "He thought that I didn't know how to use it. When he was about to attack, all I had to do was think about fire again — and it worked!"

I glanced down at the knife in my hand . . . and got another surprise.

It was my *pocketknife!* Moments ago, I'd held the large, powerful knife in my hand. Now, it had returned to the same old folding pocketknife that I'd bought! The long, shiny blade was gone, and the white skull at the bottom of the handle was gone. It was just an ordinary knife.

I was going to miss not being the King of Fire.

✳ ✳ ✳

Somehow, we were able to find the campfire that we had started earlier in the night. There were still a few glowing embers, and with some dry leaves and branches we were able to get the fire going again.

Bobby finally fell asleep, his head laying on Erin's leg as she sat by the fire. I was tired, too.

But we were still lost. We were still lost in the wilds, and had no idea how to get back to camp. The only thing we could do was wait. We would wait by the fire until morning, and then maybe we could find our way back to our camp site.

But let me tell you, I had an eerie feeling as I glanced at the dark shadows around us! I kept thinking I would see spirits peering back at me.

Erin fell asleep, and I finally dozed off, too.

But not for long.

I don't know what caused me to wake up, but when I did, I knew instantly that something was wrong. I looked around at the dark trees around us, but I didn't see anything. I looked up into the sky, but all I saw was the dark sky and billions of stars. I turned and looked into the fire. As I gazed into the burning flames, I began to see it. Erin saw it, too.

A face.

33

There was no mistake.

A face was forming in the fire. I could see it swirling in the flames, twisting and turning. It grew higher and began to form in the billowing gray smoke.

Suddenly it raised above the fire, and I recognized the face.

It was the old Indian! And he was *smiling!*

"You have done well," his voice boomed. "Very well, indeed."

"Uh, thanks," I said. "But we still have a problem. We're still just as lost as we were earlier. We need to—"

Before I could finish my sentence, the old Indian began to fade away.

"No!" Wait!" I shouted. "I'm sorry!

Whatever I said . . . I'm sorry! Come back! Help us out of the forest!"

But it was too late. The old Indian was gone. I could only watch helplessly as the gray smoke wisped up into the dark sky above.

All at once the fire began to grow . . . and grow, and grow and GROW!

"Erin!" I screamed, leaping to my feet. "Help! The whole forest is going to be set fire!"

Bobby awoke and Erin jumped up. The flames towered into the night sky.

"What do we do?!?!" she shouted over the roaring fire. "We don't have any water or anything!"

I started kicking sand over the flames, hoping that would help. I used a stick and pulled apart some of the burning logs. Erin threw dirt on the fire. Even Bobby helped. It took several minutes, but we were finally able to get the flames back down to a safer level.

Whew! That was a close one! I thought we were going to burn down the forest.

Erin sat back down by the fire, and Bobby fell asleep again. I was wide awake after all of the commotion, and I stared into the flames and thought about everything that had happened.

I had so many questions—questions that I was sure would never be answered. What had happened to the strange six-toed bear that had disappeared when we found it? Where had the Old Indian come from? Where had he gone? Was Avan-Dar gone for good?

Yes.

Of all my questions, I knew the answer to that one. Avan-Dar had been defeated, and all of the creatures of the Underforest could now live in peace. I took a deep breath, yawned, and soon fell asleep.

But not for long.

I was awakened abruptly by a noise. I snapped my head up, looking at the flickering gloom around us.

Crunch.

There it was again.

Crunch.

It was coming closer!

I heard two more loud snaps—and then a dark form appeared in the shadows!

34

My heart raced like a locomotive. Blood surged through my veins like rocket fuel.

I reached for my pocketknife.

Crunch. The dark form took a step closer.

"There you are!" a deep voice suddenly boomed out.

I didn't need to hear anything more. I recognized the voice before he even finished the sentence.

Dad!

Boy, was I glad to see him! And Mom was right behind him!

"You found us!" I shouted, springing from the ground. My shout awoke Erin and Bobby, and they both leapt up, too.

We had been found. We were safe.

* * *

I don't think I need to go into details about just how much trouble I got into. Let's just say that there are a lot of things I *won't* be doing for the rest of the summer.

And I had lost my outdoor survival manual. I was certain that it was somewhere in the forest where we had started the campfire, but I couldn't go look for it now.

Bummer.

But we were safe. Dad and Mom had found us, and we made it back to camp. Mom said that they were just about ready to call the police and report us missing. That's when they found us.

The next morning, I kind of kept to myself. Dad was pretty mad at me, and I figured I'd better just watch what I was doing and try to get back on his good side.

But I was curious. I wanted to know how they had found us. So I asked him.

"The fire," he answered, as he packed up one of the tents. "You built that big fire, and we saw the flames from a long way off. We knew it had to be the three of you."

It was then that I realized what the old Indian

had done! He was the one who had made the fire grow like it did. He made it big so that Mom and Dad would see it!

The old Indian had saved us.

Later in the day, Dad admitted to me that he was proud of the way we handled the situation. He said that we didn't panic, which was the right thing to do. We'd kept clear heads, and we survived the night because of it.

Of course, there were a lot of other things we had survived . . . but he'd never believe those things! Bobby had told them all about what had happened, but Mom just rolled her eyes and told him that he had been dreaming.

We packed up our gear later that day and continued on through the forest, until we found another spot to camp. We roasted marshmallows around the fire, caught fireflies, and went to bed. I wondered if I would find tracks in our campsite in the morning. If I did, you can bet I wasn't going to follow them! After a few moments, I fell asleep.

I don't know what time it was, because it was still dark . . . but I was awakened by a terrible shrieking in the night! I could hear commotion in the camp, and screaming!

I smiled, snuggled in my sleeping bag. I

could hear Mom hollering at Dad—he had pitched the tent on another ant's nest.

I fell back to sleep, still smiling, listening to Mom and Dad holler and shout as they swatted the tiny bugs off each other.

35

The problem with vacations is that they're just too short. It seemed like we had only started camping when it was time to go home.

We did get to stay another day, however. The night we tried to leave was too windy, and the Mackinac Bridge was closed! If the weather is bad, sometimes the bridge gets closed. Anyway, it was really windy that night, so we got to stay in a motel in St. Ignace. Which was kind of cool, because it was right near the water. Erin and I got to go down to the lake and skip rocks, and then we all went out to eat at a restaurant. Man . . . camping is fun, and it's great to roast hot dogs and things, but restaurant food is a lot better!

The next day was clear and sunny, and we started out early. The Mackinac Bridge had re-opened during the night, and we began our journey south. But we wouldn't actually be going home until tomorrow. Dad said that we were going to visit Grandma and Grandpa in Kalamazoo before we went home.

That would be fun. Grandpa and Grandma have a big house, and I've spent a lot of time there. Erin and I have even met a few friends in the area.

I fell asleep right around Grayling, and I didn't wake up until we were in Kalamazoo! I must've slept for hours.

Grandma and Grandpa were waiting, and Grandma was working on a big dinner for all of us. We still had a couple of hours before it would be ready, so Erin and Bobby and I went outside to see if we could track down a few of the other kids that we know. We only get to Kalamazoo about once a month, but we know a lot of other people on the block. We've been coming to visit Grandma and Grandpa in Kalamazoo for as long as I can remember.

We walked around the block and didn't find anyone, but on the next block we got a surprise. I could hear carnival music! The fair was in town!

We ran up the street and skipped through a couple of yards and sure enough, we could see the carnival set up in the distance. There were big red and white canvas tents, and whirling, twirling colorful rides.

"Let's go!" Bobby pleaded.

"Yeah, let's!" Erin agreed, her voice alive with excitement. "We have lots of time before dinner!"

We had just started walking toward the carnival when all of a sudden a shout came from between two houses!

"Erin! Kevin!" someone yelled. I spun, and smiled, recognizing Kayleigh and Andy Fisher. We haven't seen them since last summer.

"Hey guys!" I shouted, waving. We walked toward them, and they met us at the sidewalk.

"How's it going?" Andy asked. We talked for few minutes. I told Kayleigh and Andy that we had been camping in St. Ignace, and we had stopped in Kalamazoo to visit and have dinner with our grandparents.

"We're going to the carnival," Bobby said, pointing to the colorful rides and tents in the distance.

A look of horror came over Kayleigh and Andy's faces. They looked shocked.

"What's wrong?" I asked. Andy and

Kayleigh began to shake their heads.

"Well, I guess it's okay to go there now," Andy said. "Now that the Klowns are gone." His voice was tense and serious.

Huh? What was the big deal about clowns? Every carnival had clowns.

"What about the clowns?" I asked.

Andy and Kayleigh looked at each other, then back at us.

"I guess we can tell you now," Kayleigh answered. "But you're not going to believe it."

"Well, after what we just went through in St. Ignace," I said, "I'd probably believe just about anything."

"Good," Andy said, nodding. "Because this is crazy. It's crazy . . . but it's true. We know. But meet us back here tonight, and we'll tell you all about the Kreepy Klowns. The Kreepy Klowns of Kalamazoo."

**Next in the 'Michigan Chillers'
series . . . .
#7 : 'Kreepy Klowns of Kalamazoo'
Go to the next page for a few
chilling chapters!**

I've always loved carnivals. *Always.* Ferris wheels, games, the smell of nachos and hot dogs, and the excited shouts and shrieks that fill the air on a hot summer day. I love everything about carnivals.

Except the clowns.

Oh, I used to like clowns. I thought they were kind of funny the way they were always goofing off and squirting everyone with water. I thought clowns were fun.

Not anymore. Not after what I just went through.

I'm Kayleigh. Kayleigh Fisher. I'm eleven, but I'll be twelve really soon. I have a brother named Andy, but I usually don't admit it. He's a goof. Not always, but most of the time. He's a year younger than me, and when he's not acting like a complete goof-off, we hang out together.

We live in Kalamazoo, Michigan. If you ever come to Kalamazoo, you're bound to see billboards on the side of the highway that say 'Kalamazoo . . . Sounds Like Fun.'

That's true. We sure do have a lot of fun here in Kalamazoo.

Until the carnival came to town. Until the Klowns showed up. Yes, that's 'Klowns' with a 'K'. Soon, you'll know why its spelled like that.

The big, colorful tents seemed to arrive overnight. Within one single day, the fairgrounds had been turned into a huge arcade of fun. Flyers had been up all over the city talking about carnival week. And the carnival was going to open on the day of my birthday! What fun. My friends and I had been saving money for over a month. We couldn't wait.

One morning when I went outside, I saw a line of big semi-trucks drive by. They were all different colors, and on the sides of the trailers, colorful carnival scenes had been painted.

Seeing them arrive, my blood started pumping. *They're here!* I thought. *They're finally here!*

As the semi-trucks rolled on past, I stood on the sidewalk and waved. Some of them honked their horns as they went by. My blood pumped harder and I got more and more excited with every arriving truck—until I saw who—or what—was driving them.

They were circus clowns! Circus clowns were driving the semi-trucks. They all had white face-paint and different colored hair. Some clowns had orange hair, some had green or yellow. They looked silly.

But there was something wrong with these clowns. I couldn't put my finger on it, but these clowns just didn't look . . . well . . . *normal.* These clowns looked scary. Scary . . . and *mean.*

They all waved at me as they headed for the fairgrounds, but I stopped waving when one of them looked at me. He smiled, but it just didn't seem to be a happy smile. The clown looked like he was angry. Oh, he was smiling, all right. But he still looked angry. His eyes were big and round, and he was glaring at me. He looked spooky.

The convoy finally passed on and I threw away my suspicious thoughts.

Sheesh, Kayleigh, I thought. *Don't be ridiculous. They're circus clowns. Circus clowns are supposed to make you happy.*

I ran back to the house and pushed away my thoughts about crazy clowns. After all, the carnival was in town! It wouldn't be long now. Soon, the air would be filled with the delicious aroma of cotton candy, elephant ears, and popcorn. Kids would be laughing and screaming as they whirled about on the dazzling rides. Bells would ring and happy calliope music would drift across the city. For the next week, my friends and my brother and I would almost *live* at the carnival. The next week would be nothing but non-stop fun.

Or so I thought.

Today was Friday. Tomorrow was my birthday. And tomorrow, the carnival would open.

The nightmare was about to begin.

2

The next morning, my brother woke me up. In the summer, I like to sleep in late. *Really* late. I like to get up right around the crack of noon.

"Happy birthday, Kayleigh!" he shouted from the doorway of my bedroom. "It's almost eleven! Come on! The carnival will be open in an hour!"

He didn't have to tell me twice. I ran a brush through my dark brown hair and got dressed. In less than ten minutes we had both polished off a bowl of *Cap'n Crunch* and were out the door.

We were off and on our way. The carnival was in town! What fun. I'm not sure what I liked better: the carnival, or my birthday.

Hooray! I was twelve. Almost a teenager. *Almost.*

As soon as we rounded our block, we could see the fairgrounds in the distance. Striped tents and brightly colored rides jutted up into the blue sky like wide, fat skyscrapers. Nothing was moving yet, since the carnival didn't officially open till noon.

Andy and I walked quickly along the sidewalk, almost breaking into a run. Mom and Dad had given me ten dollars as an early birthday present so I'd have money for the rides. I had stuffed the money into the pocket of my jeans. I had a ten-dollar bill, a few one-dollar bills, and a bunch of quarters. The quarters jingled as I walked.

Finally, we made it to the fairgrounds. A tall, wire fence goes around the whole area, and the main gate was still closed. There was already a line of people waiting to get in.

I looked at my watch. It was 11:30. We still had another half hour before the carnival would open.

We stood in line and waited for a few

minutes. More and more people began to arrive, and we saw a few of our friends. Families brought their children, boys brought their girlfriends, girls brought their boyfriends. A lot of people were all waiting to be the first inside.

"Hey Kayleigh," Andy suddenly whispered. He spoke quietly so no one else nearby could hear him. *"I know a place around back where we could see what's going on. Wanna go check it out?"*

"You mean sneak into the carnival?!?!" I said. That was not something I wanted to do.

"Of course not!" he hissed. *"But the tents are right by the fence! We can get real close to the rides and the tents and see what's going on before anyone else."*

I have to admit, that sounded fun. But we'd lose our place in line. Nevertheless, I agreed to go with him. It would be fun to see everything close up, and before anyone else.

We stepped out of line and followed the fence as it wound around the big field. Tents and rides towered above us, just on the other side of the fence. We were so close, we could have reached out and touched some of the steel beams that held up the rides.

Soon, we came to a tent that had been set up right next to the fence. It was red and white striped, and it was right near the rear entrance of the fairgrounds. This was the entrance that was used by the semi-trucks to unload all of their equipment. It was a private entrance, to be used by the carnival workers only.

And the gate was open!

Did we dare?

No, we shouldn't. We shouldn't, and we wouldn't. Sneaking into the carnival would get us into a lot of trouble.

We stopped walking and looked around. Suddenly a clown came into view! He was walking between two trucks, then he turned and went into a tent.

"Andy," I whispered, raising my arm. *"Look at that tent."*

Andy looked to where I was pointing. The clown had gone through the opening of the tent and was no longer in site. Above the opening of the tent was a big, hand-painted sign that read:

KLOWNS ONLY - ALL OTHERS KEEP OUT

Someone had better give the clowns some spelling lessons. 'Clowns' is supposed to be spelled with the letter C, not a K.

"That must be where they put their make-up on," Andy said. He turned his head and shot me a sneaky grin. "Wanna go see how the clowns put on their make-up?" he asked.

That would be cool!

But no. We'd have to go through the rear entrance, and we'd get in trouble for sure. And besides . . . I suddenly remembered seeing the clowns yesterday, and the strange looks they all had on their faces. Now I wasn't sure if I wanted to see the clowns, after all.

"Look over there," Andy said, pointing. "There's a tear in the side of the tent! It's right by the fence! We can walk over there and peek through from this side of the fence! We don't even have to sneak inside!"

I was going to say no, that we should just

go back and wait in line. But when Andy started walking along the fence toward the tent, I followed.

After all . . . we *were* on the other side of the fence. We weren't doing anything wrong. How could we get into trouble?

We walked quietly to where the rip in the tent was. The tear was only about six inches long, but it was wide enough to see through. I leaned forward, my face almost pressing against the mesh wire fence.

I was peering through the rip in the canvas when a movement close by, from inside, caught my attention.

It was a shadow. The looming shadow of a clown against the canvas tent. It was dark, and I could clearly see his form as he moved.

He stopped just a few feet from where we were. All we could see was his silhouette, but it was easy to see all of his features: His arms, his legs, his head, and his curly hair.

But it was what was in his hand that made me almost scream in horror.

The clown was holding a knife.

3

We stayed as still as we could. I didn't even breathe. I was afraid to. I thought that if I took a breath, the clown would hear me. My heart was doing flip-flops in my chest, and I was almost certain that the clown would hear that for sure.

Had the clown spotted us? Had he heard us? He was right near the edge of the tent, gripping the knife tightly in his hand. It looked like he was staring right at us. Maybe he could see our shadows like we could see his shadow.

Right beside me, Andy was motionless. His eyes were fixed on the huge clown shadow only a few feet from us. Neither of us moved.

Then the clown began walking away from

the side of the tent. Whew! He hadn't seen us, after all.

Andy leaned forward and peered through the rip in the tent.

"For gosh sakes," he whispered quietly. I could hear the relief in his voice. *"The clown is holding a butter knife! He's making a sandwich!"*

I almost started to laugh. *Of course,* I thought. *That's all it was. A butter knife.* I felt silly, thinking that it would have been anything else.

I was relieved, but I still felt uneasy. I couldn't put my finger on it, but the clowns made me nervous. I just didn't like the way they looked at me yesterday. I know it sounds crazy, but something told me that I needed to watch out for the clowns.

These clowns, anyway.

I glanced down at my watch. It was 11:55.

"Come on!" I urged Andy. "It's almost time to go inside!"

Reluctantly, he drew away from the fence and stood up. We walked back to the main entrance where a huge crowd of people had gathered. Kids were screaming and laughing, parents were chattering, and smiles were everywhere. We had to get in the back of the line, but I didn't care. I was too excited.

Suddenly, carnival music filled the air. Rides slowly began to squeak and move, slowly at first, then faster. The air was electric and filled with excitement. The crowd around us let out a cheer, and a wave of applause swept through. Andy and I clapped our hands. The roar of applause and cheering was deafening.

The gates opened up, and the crowd began to move slowly forward.

The carnival was opening! The carnival was opening, and hundreds — even thousands — of people were coming. They were coming to ride the rides and play the games. They were coming to gorge themselves on hot dogs and candy and popcorn and all kinds of scrumptious food. They were coming to have fun, just like we were.

Of course, the clowns had other plans.

The line moved quickly, and soon we were at the gate. I dug into my pocket for my money to buy tickets.

When I looked up and saw the clown, I gasped. Clowns were selling tickets! I hadn't seen them before, but there were five or six of them. They sat in ticket booths and sold tickets to people. They looked like the same clowns that were driving the semi-trucks yesterday.

Andy was behind me. "Come on," he prodded. "You're holding up the line."

But I couldn't move. I just stared at the clown. I stared at the clown, and the clown stared back at me. He didn't say anything. He didn't move. He just gazed at me with cold, dark eyes.

And his *smile.*

He was smiling, but it didn't look like a happy smile. It was more of a sneer, like he was all smug and had something to hide. I didn't like the way he looked at all.

Then I noticed something else. *All of the other clowns had the same, strange look on their faces.* They were smiling, but, they all had this cold, dead stare as they took money and exchanged tickets.

"Kayleigh," Andy persisted from behind me. He nudged my shoulder. "Come on! Give him your money!"

I managed to reach out and hand my money to the clown, but I snapped my arm back quickly so I wouldn't touch his hand. He never took his eyes off of mine while he pulled out a strip of yellow tickets and handed them back to me.

I reached out to take the tickets — and he grabbed my wrist!

I would have screamed, but my breath was gone. I couldn't even get my mouth open.

I was horrified. The clown's grasp on my wrist was tight and firm. He had wiry, strong hands, and I don't think I could have struggled free if I tried.

The clown leaned closer. I could feel his hand pulling on my arm, pulling me closer, pulling me toward him.

"Enjoy the rides," he wheezed. *"Enjoy the rides . . . ."* His voice was low and gruff, like an animal's growl. His smile grew wider, exposing crooked, yellow teeth. His grip loosened, and I finally yanked my hand from his grasp. I spun and walked hurriedly past Andy and stopped a few feet away.

"What's up with you?" Andy turned and asked me. Then he turned back around and faced the ticket window, handing the clown his money. In a moment, he was stuffing the wad of tickets into his pocket. He strode over to me.

"Didn't you notice anything different about that clown?" I asked him. He turned and looked back at the ticket booth, then turned and faced me. He had a dumbfounded look on his face.

"No," he replied, shaking his head. "Like, what?"

"I don't know," I answered nervously. "But he just didn't seem . . . well, you know . . . *normal.*"

"He's a circus clown, Kayleigh," Andy snickered. "He's not *supposed* to be normal."

"Yeah, but—"

"Let's go," he interrupted, turning his attention to the rides that were whirling about. He started walking toward the colorful midway.

I couldn't help but take one more glance at the strange clown in the ticket booth. It was like I could sense him watching me, glaring at me from his chair. I turned to look at him, to prove to myself that he *wasn't* looking at me.

But he was!

He was staring at me with that same, awful grin.

And his mouth was moving! He wasn't speaking, not out loud anyway. But just the same, I could understand him. I watched his lips move, and I could understand what he was saying.

Enjoy the rides, he mouthed. *Enjoy the rides
. . . .*

I turned and ran as fast as I could,
bumping into people as I tried to catch up with
Andy. The clown's voice kept rolling through
my head.

Enjoy the rides, it repeated, over and over
and over in that deep, throaty growl. *Enjoy the
rides . . . .*

Something was very, very wrong at the
carnival. Very wrong. Why I stayed, I'll never
know. I think it was because that deep down, I
was hoping I was mistaken. I was hoping that
the dark feeling I had, the feeling that was balled
up in my gut like a knot, was nothing but my
own imagination running away with me.

I was hoping that I was wrong about the
clowns.

But I wasn't wrong—and I knew it. And
it wasn't going to take very long to find out that
my worst fears were about to come true.

STRANGE SPIRITS OF ST. IGNACE WORD SEARCH!

```
Z J Z T F X D N H U W Q X D R I H S Y W
J Q W M K J X J P H U P R F Y K T X P U
G S Q U W E Y T L G K S V W C Z E M E R
F Z L N X X B A C L R M V Z D B I M J S
M X B U C L V Z N N V D C C D C X O Q J
Y O D N O A Y C R A W H K X H H H L N U
Y K V N N O M V D I C U R I E N Y E W A
B E D D G W W P L D E S G D A S V S S A
E Z A H V B W R F N P A N T J U R A U P
A R J T V C Q D S I N E H X N Y O B O F
Z N I H N F M H R C R A V D A J E C A R
Q Z F N E E D I H I N E E Y Q A K W L S
S Q W P J B T I F R O R B R R E Q G G K
M T V W Q S L F A T F B Q T T W K C F L
K A I Z T L O N G O O O R K L D Q A J J
T E C G E G D I R B C A N I K C A M T U
U E V R N A E E N B C I K F P V Y P W C
B D S I E A S R M K F S U J C D U I C G
D T K M N T C O S E Y B Z C W V E N H K
O U U O M P L E Y L C E A M D U O G E A
```

St. Ignace
Spirits
Underforest
Kevin
Erin
Bobby
Mackinac Bridge
Camping
King of Fire

Pocketknife
Avan-Dar
Campfire
Indian
Moles
Bear Tracks
Tent
Michigan Chillers
Johnathan Rand

WORD SCRAMBLE!

Unscramble the words and place the new words in the blanks!

ts geanic   __ _____

getsarn   _____

nkvei   _____

aiigmnch   _____

ntnhojaha dnra   _____ ____

pmngaic   _____

refi   ____

yobbb   _____

ecofkkptnie   _____

ftusrnrdeoe   _____

isitrsp   _____

soeml   _____

clsrileh   _____

kncmicaa irdegb   _____ _____

ABOUT THE AUTHOR

Johnathan Rand is the author of more than 50 books, with well over 2 million copies in print. Series include **AMERICAN CHILLERS, MICHIGAN CHILLERS, FREDDIE FERNORTNER, FEARLESS FIRST GRADER,** and **THE ADVENTURE CLUB.** He's also co-authored a novel for teens (with Christopher Knight) entitled **PANDEMIA.** When not traveling, Rand lives in northern Michigan with his wife and two dogs. He is also the only author in the world to have a store that sells only his works: **CHILLERMANIA!** is located in Indian River, Michigan. Johnathan Rand is not always at the store, but he has been known to drop by frequently. Find out more at:

www.americanchillers.com

join the official

AMERICAN CHILLERS

FAN CLUB!

**Visit
www.americanchillers.com
for details!**

Also by Johnathan Rand:

GHOST IN THE GRAVEYARD

AMERICAN CHILLERS
PICTURE PAGES!

Chiller fans!

AMERICAN CHILLERS
PICTURE PAGES!

Johnathan & Mrs. Rand, arriving in style for a book
signing at Barnes & Noble, Saginaw, Michigan!

AMERICAN CHILLERS
PICTURE PAGES!

With Debra Gantz at Hickory Woods Elementary!

AMERICAN CHILLERS
PICTURE PAGES!

Getting out the scare at Ann Arbor Public Library!

AMERICAN CHILLERS
PICTURE PAGES!

Chilling out at Pattengill Elementary!

AMERICAN CHILLERS
PICTURE PAGES!

A sellout performance at Roseville Public Library!

AMERICAN CHILLERS
PICTURE PAGES!

A warm welcome at Eastlawn Elementary!

For information on personal appearances, motivational speaking engagements, or book signings, write to:

AudioCraft Publishing, Inc.
PO Box 281
Topinabee Island, MI 49791

or call
(231) 238-0297

Johnathan Rand travels internationally for school visits and book signings! For booking information, call:

1 (231) 238-0338!